Praise for the Great Thirst Serial:

"The action part of the story barely begins in this first part, but I laughed out loud in places ... "

"... A great start to a great serial novel. I loved the characters their quirks and particularities."

"I enjoyed the whole thing and am excited to read the whole series."

"It is an exciting read and ... [pulls you along] ... enthralled"

The Great Thirst
Part Four: Persecuted
A Serial Archaeological Mystery

by

Mary C. Findley

Findley Family Video Publications

The Great Thirst Part Four: Persecuted – A Serial Archeological Mystery

by Mary C. Findley

"Speaking the truth in love."

In Association with The Edge Books

What is THE EDGE?

THE EDGE is a conviction. It's where we stand to save the lost. It's stepping away from our comfortable pews to bring God to the world. It's following Jesus' example to minister to the outcasts, the overlooked, the forgotten.

THE EDGE is about relationship, not religion. It's God's power being stronger and God's love running deeper than anything people face. It's being fearless in the face of adversity and willing to look the devil in the eye and say, "You can't have him or her anymore."

We are authors, Christians, people walking by faith. We are THE EDGE.

www.TheEdgeBooks.blogspot.com

Acknowledgments

Cover credits: Book Four: Images from Canstock, Deposit Photo, and Pixabay

Background texture from pixabay.com, by user Zeana

Artifact image from http://www.fouman.com/ Iranian Historical Photo Gallery source for Darius I Persepolis Gold Plates

These plates were found by archeologists in 1938, in Persepolis, near modern day Shiraz, Iran. There were two gold plates and two silver plates in a stone box, written on in cuneiform script. The plates date to 518 – 515 BC.

Tesla Roadster (chapter header image) 13 April 2010 Author Thomas Doerfer Wikimedia Commons

Fingers with dust (section divider image) from pixabay.com user Unsplash

One Night With the King is a movie mentioned several times in the series. Released 2006 in the United States, it is based on the novel *Hadassah: One Night with the King* by Tommy Tenney and Mark Andrew Olsen. It is a dramatization of the biblical story of Esther, who risked her life by approaching the king to request that he save the Jewish people. The movie was produced by Matt Crouch and Laurie Crouch of Gener8Xion Entertainment

Table of Contents

"Behold, days are coming,

declares the Lord God, When I will send a famine on the land, Not a famine for bread or a thirst for water, But rather for hearing the words of the Lord. People will stagger from sea to sea And from the north even to the east; They will go to and fro to seek the word of the Lord, But they will not find it."

Amos 8: 11-12, NASB

The Great Thirst

Chapter Forty-eight– "If You'll Just Come and Explain ..."

Life at Precious Treasure Campground never really settled into a routine. Keith learned that quite a few other people lived there, some in the main building like him and his father and grandmother, and some in cabins here and there around the property. They all had a story to tell about persecutions that were more or less subtle.

He met Larry Stokes, a pastor and his family who had lost their large, thriving church when the government had decided that the coffee shop and dramatic performance center they had on the property were for-profit enterprises and denied tax-exempt status to the entire ministry.

"Any money we made from them we used for shelters and other ministries," the man told Keith. "But they claimed we had to be hiding some of the income. Our bookkeeping accounted for every penny taken in and spent, but that didn't matter. We just couldn't keep paying the legal fees to keep fighting. Someone bought the property for back taxes and turned the church into a conference center.

"I've tried to find another church, but once a pastor gets involved in fighting the government over tax exemption and loses, no one wants him. People are scared of that big stick, and they don't want to lose that fight. Many churches just do what it takes to keep in the government's good graces. They don't want to start the fight at all."

Several people living at the compound had online ministries. "What happened to going off the grid to escape persecution?" Keith asked Talia. "These people are active online all the time. Aren't we going to get caught, doing all we're talking about doing?"

"All kinds of people pursue causes other people don't like online," Talia replied "Doomsday Preppers, Second Amendment Rights, and all kinds of political activists and religious teachers. You can protect yourself on the internet better than if you preach on a street corner or distribute pamphlets by mail. You just have to know how."

"I'm so used to talking to people face to face," Keith said. "That's why I became a teacher, because I loved seeing the kids every day – seeing their faces – putting an arm around their shoulders. It's not the same, trying to teach in an email. Even on Skype, it's weird, not being there with them. When this crazy stuff dies down, are we going to go back to teaching someplace real?"

"Like Uncle Naddy says, there are waves of persecutions. Jenny Kaine might back off, and we might get to do that. Sometimes the media has more power than the government, though. Remember that famous radio talk show host who said he'd never run for president, because he had more power just sitting behind his microphone than anybody in public office?

"He was right. You can still teach, Keith, and still change lives. We won't always be holed up here, for sure. We'll get involved with those orichalcum tablets we found, and others that are going to be found. We'll dive, and we'll dig, and we'll find more ancient tech. We'll figure out what the connection is between stuff like Britomartis's ax and the Guardians. There might be more protective devices, and devices to make spreading the Word easier and safer."

"I know. I need to be patient." Keith sighed. "Okay, I finally got all the emails of the kids from the Bible as Literature class together and I'm ready to transfer them to the secure site we set up to continue the Reclamation Project."

"Great. I've been putting out feelers to teachers and students involved in the project in other places. We didn't have much time to build relationships with them but I know some of our kids made friends through the Repository site. They are going to want to reconnect, and we should build up those contacts if there's a possibility of finding like-minded people we can encourage, and who can encourage us. You're already learning that this can be a very discouraging way to live and try to minister."

"Let's see if we can get online and finish getting things all set up to officially open the new Reclamation site," Keith said. "This was something Joana dreamed about, you know? She said we should never have waited for a government site to share the Word. Shame on us for not making this a priority ourselves."

"She was so right. Keith, what if we call the site *Joana's Sparrows*? No one will get anything suspicious out of that. But people who knew Joana will realize it's a tribute to her love for the Word and her belief that God takes care of us no matter what."

Keith didn't answer for a minute, as the realization hit him that a week ago they had sat at the table back at home right after Joana's funeral. He rubbed the back of his neck and jumped up from the console where they had just seated themselves.

"Excuse me, Talia. Sorry. I have to go outside for a few minutes." He bolted out of the room, out of the building, and into a sea of grass and wildflowers. He ran a few steps and the overpowering beauty of this place chased away that smothering grief. Mountains with a hint of snow still on the peaks made a bowl and framed the perfect blue sky and the few white clouds overhead. He turned and saw Talia standing on the porch, unsure if she should join him. He waved her over.

"Imagine Joana finally able to run free in a place that must be a million times more beautiful than this," she said softly, taking his hand.

"Yeah. I can. I did. C'mon. Time to get to work."

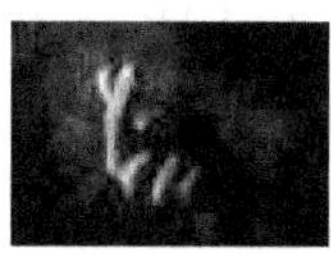

"Okay, now we have the new email set up. We can transfer the contacts over and start sending the kids the plans we made, to see how they want to participate," Talia said. "Wait. This is weird. There's already mail in the inbox."

"Let me see." Keith looked over her shoulder. "Whoa. *Ten* emails? And they're all from kids in the class."

"Oh, no!" Talia pointed to the first opened email. "Rikki sent pictures of the school. Look at all the heavy equipment. She says they're just going to bulldoze it."

"Yeah, here's one from Annie. She says the kids are going to be split up among different schools. Man, that's why they let us keep Bradley Central open in the first place. Everybody's such a long distance from another school. But why are they making them go to different schools? Are they trying to make sure they're separated?"

"Here's one from Tom. They're saying they tried to protest the bulldozing of the school. They keep asking why it won't be fixed up, but no one will answer."

"The crews are expected to begin demolition first thing Monday," Keith said. "Wait – no way. Adam says here some of the Bible as Literature class will sneak in and see if any of their stuff survived the explosion."

"They can't do that! It's got to be dangerous,"

Talia exclaimed.

"Look at this one from Jayna. She says a couple of the kids were arrested for trespassing on the school property yesterday. The police have locked them up. She said they were looking for evidence to prove it was a bomb. Talia, she says the police say they won't let them go."

Talia read aloud from the email

> *Mr. Bradley and Ms. Ramin, Sean and Daryl's mom and dad said they told the cops Mr. Bradley told them it was a bomb that exploded at the school. The cops told them no, it was just a water heater. Daryl said Sean argued with them and said the government was lying to shut down the school.*
>
> *The cops asked them if Mr. Bradley told them to say that. They said no, but the cops said Mr. Bradley would have to come and give a statement to prove he didn't. That was the only way they were gonna let Daryl and Sean out.*
>
> *Mr. Bradley, everybody in town is talking about how your whole family disappeared right after the bomb went off. People are starting to say you might have had something to do with it. We know it's not true, but now those two guys are in jail, and their parents say the cops want to talk to you, and they're holding them as – Daryl's dad says it's called* material witnesses *– until you come and straighten it out. He says they can hold them forever.*

"I have to go back to town," Keith said.

"You can't," Talia cried. "They'll just arrest you instead."

"No, they won't," Keith scoffed. "I'll explain about the van following us, and how we were afraid for my grandmother. Clark knows about the van. He'll back me up."

"But Keith, they can jail you just because we never reported the accident we witnessed with the van. What if they blame us for the crash? This is a trap, don't you see? They want you back in town so they can get you. They'll make up anything to hold you, and you'll be back in Jenny Kaine's power."

"What am I supposed to do? Those two kids are in jail because of me. The other kids are going to get themselves arrested or hurt when they try to go into the school before it's plowed under. I have to talk them out of that. This is what I was saying about being there in person. I stay here, hiding, I look guilty and I have no way to stop those kids. Nobody's going to listen to an email."

"You can't go back to town. We can't allow you get yourself arrested. We need you to help with the work on the Testaments. I need you to be safe and alive to marry me."

Keith stared at her, clenching his fists. "Those kids need me, too. And what do you mean you 'can't allow' me to do what I need to do? Are you going to knock me down like you did that fake security guy? Like you did Dan? Is Naddy going to lock me up in one of these buildings that I haven't even seen the inside of yet?"

Chapter Forty-nine – "We're All in this Together"

Talia stared up at him. "Where is this coming from? I've done nothing but protect you and try to help you see what believers all over the world face every day. I am not your enemy. I don't know why I should even have to tell you that."

She shot out of her chair and ran out of the room. Keith stood there for a full minute before taking off to find his dad. Joshua Bradley sat in the large, open community area of the main building, drinking coffee with several other men and women.

"Hey, Dad," Keith said, forcing what he hoped looked like a genuine smile. "Can I have the keys to the van?"

"The keys to the van? What for?" his dad asked.

"I just want to go for a drive. Cabin fever, I guess."

"Lots of room to walk around the compound," a man said as he took a sip of his coffee. "Pretty place. Always something new to explore. Even driving space. It's pretty big."

"I need to get out," Keith said, trying to keep his tone level. "Can I please have the keys, Dad?"

His father looked up at him. "Where are you going, Keith?"

Keith looked around. No one had moved or spoken except Joshua. "Could we ... talk someplace else?"

"We're all in this together, son," an elderly man said, standing and offering a hand. Keith shook it woodenly. ""I'm Bart Matthews. This is my wife Sheila. We ran the Truth Adventures theme park in Nevada, until they shut us down. Maybe you heard about it."

"I'm ... not sure ... wait ... the one that got sued for child endangerment?" Keith asked.

"That's the one." Bart smiled wanly. "We had exhibits of people and dinosaurs together, among other things, and the local school district complained. Some parents brought their kids to the park and the kids used pictures they took and our literature in reports they gave for classes. We were accused of teaching dangerous and false information. Still trying to figure out how it's dangerous, except to them, of course.

"But I spent 18 months in jail, and my exhibits were seized. We were able to get them back, and though some of them were in rough shape, they are stored here in one of the warehouses." As he talked, his whole body stiffened and the woman sitting beside him reached up and grabbed his hand. He relaxed slowly and seated himself.

"Eighteen months in jail?" Keith echoed. The couple nodded.

"We lost our house, basically for having a Bible study," a young woman said. "Sorry. I'm Fran Taylor." She popped up out of her seat, as did all the men, and Keith shook hands with her, too. "My husband Saul lost his job with the city over it. They demanded a property reassessment and cited us for parking violations, failing to get a permit ... He had trouble getting another job, and they fined us for being late trying to pay the fines, and then we couldn't make the mortgage payments ... well ... he's in cancer treatments now, and I had no place to go."

"Son," Joshua Bradley said, "if there's something you're concerned about, beyond what I already know, please tell me. Tell *us*. We can't let the enemy divide us when there's a possibility someone may have the knowledge to help us solve the problem."

Keith dropped into a chair and the content of the emails from the Bible as Literature class spilled out of him. He took a deep, unsteady breath when he finished.

"Brad Shannon," said the lady whose husband had cancer.

"Who?" Keith asked.

"Of course!" Joshua Bradley exclaimed. "Brad Shannon! He's just the person we need!"

"Who's Brad Shannon?" Keith persisted.

"You don't remember that lawyer who tried to harass the school courtesy of the Holdens?" his father smiled. "He used to work for the Civil Rights Defense Association."

"Oh, the guy who came to church and talked about Jonathan Edwards?" Keith said.

"It was *your* church?" Fran Taylor beamed. "Now he's with the Constitutional Protection Legal Foundation. Attorney Shannon's probably the only reason we didn't go to jail. He said they're starting to revisit the idea of debtors' prisons. He's had legal troubles of his own, since leaving the CRDA, but he says he won't stop helping other people. You need to call him. He has a special secure line, and answers it personally." She pushed a business card across the table.

"Let's go make that call," Joshua said, rising and putting a hand on Keith's back.

"Okay, Dad, in just a minute. First of all I have to go see if I can get my foot out of my mouth with Talia."

"Oh, was that why she ran through here like the world ended?" Joshua sighed. "The two of you have got to learn to face the world together, Son. The enemy is out there, not between you."

"Yeah," Keith muttered. "Yeah. Which way did she go?"

Everyone pointed up the main staircase. "Her room is at the head of the stairs," Sheila Matthews said with a smile. "Number 101."

Keith nodded and set off up the stairs at a run. He stood on one foot, then the other, and rocked back and forth for a minute.

"Just knock!" Everyone downstairs called out.

Talia's door opened before he could make a fist. She stared at him with puffy red eyes. "I heard someone yelling," she said.

"They were yelling at me for being an idiot," Keith said. "Talia, I'm sorry. You keep saying I can handle everything you throw at me, but I didn't handle that right at all. Please forgive me. Dad said the enemy is out there. It's gotta be you and me against the world, right?"

Talia had taken a good look down at the interested parties at the coffee table and Keith sighed when that *spring-into-his-arms* expression faded off her face.

"I overreacted, too," Talia said softly, knitting her fingers together.

"C'mon. Dad and I are going to call that lawyer who got saved at our church. People are saying he can help with the kids."

"Oh!" Talia caught her breath. "Oh, yes! Brad Shannon! I forgot all about him. That's a wonderful idea!"

"Why does everybody know this guy but me?" Keith complained as they ran down the stairs together.

"Material witness has become a real, true, hostage-taking and extortion tactic for law enforcement," Attorney Shannon said when they connected with him on a teleconference call. He rubbed his brief red bead and stared at the ceiling. "I can file paperwork that should get those two kids out of jail pretty quick. But we have to move fast on the other matter, and keep those kids off the school site. It's dangerous physically and legally. Their loyalty to the program and to you is not helpful in this particular case. It makes you look like some kind of cult leader."

"But I'm sure I can talk some sense into them," Keith said. "I've known them all their lives. They'll listen to me."

"No way should you go down there, Keith. That's exactly what whoever's trying to pull this stunt wants. And it's bad from a practical standpoint, too, because it romanticizes the 'cause' in their minds. They see you as a fugitive from oppressive government, risking everything to encourage followers. They might even believe you pulled a Robin Hood and are responsible for the bombing. We can't let that thinking continue. They'll just get more thrills out of taking risks themselves."

"I didn't think of it like that," Keith admitted.

"Of course you didn't. That's a mistake good-hearted people make all the time, though. You're only concerned about the safety of the kids. But they got themselves into this, and they're making your situation worse by their actions. Somebody needs to make them aware of that. Who would the kids trust, though? I don't think any of them would know me. I'm just a sleazy lawyer, anyway."

Talia turned her head as they heard the *new email* signal, musical tones different from the camel bell ringtone but still oriental in sound. "Excuse me. That's the account the kids are using. I need to see if there's been a new development." She slid over to check the mail.

"My dad's in just as much danger as I am, right? He can't go either?" Keith asked Brad.

"Maybe not quite as much danger for him, but I'd say no, he shouldn't go either," Brad replied.

"Certainly not Ms. Ramin. Who do you really trust down there? Somebody local, a person everybody knows, and whom the kids respect but don't ... well .. The only word I can think of is worship? Somebody who can bring them back down to earth."

"Sam Ewing," Talia said, and burst out laughing.

Chapter Fifty – Sam Ewing Saves the Day

"Sam?" Keith repeated. "What makes you think he –"

"Because he just emailed us in the Restoration account," Talia said. "Look at all these typos! He said he's never typed on a computer before in his life. But he says ... I think ..." she squinted and stared at the screen "... he says his aunt told him to do something about those crazy kids to get them to stop their foolishness. He wants to know if it's okay to execute his plan – or – I guess it's his aunt's plan."

"Dr. Ewing and Sam have a plan to calm the kids down?" Keith stared blankly at the messy email.

"Okay, sounds like you've got possibilities, anyway," Brad said. "Let me get going on the paperwork to get those kids released and do what I can to quash the rumors flying about the Mad Bradley Bombers."

"Thanks," Keith said.

"Thank you so much," Talia added.

They signed off the conference call and turned to stare at Sam Ewing's email.

"Do you think he knows about his aunt being a Guardian of the Testaments?" Keith asked. "I can't believe Sam wrote this. It looks like he typed with his toes."

"I'm guessing Sam doesn't know the real reason his aunt wants him to do this, but it's true that the kids all love him, in spite of how he rubs the grownups the wrong way. He's got such a rebel attitude but a true heart." Talia smiled. "I think he's the perfect one to pull this off. Do you think their plan will work?"

"Tell him to go ahead and let 'er rip," Keith said with a grin. "I wish I could see the kids' faces. They are going to love this."

"They made the news," Joshua Bradley said Monday morning as he carried coffees into Keith and Talia's war room. "Oh, I see you found it."

Keith pulled a chair closer so he could sit with them.

"Controversy continues to grow over the mysterious events at tiny Bradley Central School," a newscaster said. "Just over a week ago a terrifying explosion rocked this school and community, shattering windows in the Shady Rest Senior Apartments across the street. Conflicting reports emerged concerning the cause of the blast. Building inspectors deemed the school too badly damaged to be salvaged and demolition was supposed to begin today."

The reporter looked behind and to her left and the camera followed as she stepped in front of the smoke-blackened exterior of Bradley Central. She pushed her microphone at Sam Ewing in a hard hat and dust-smeared clothing. He beat on his pants and the reporter coughed and backed up, frantically trying to rescue her perfect dark blue ensemble.

"Oh, how original." Talia groaned. Father and son burst out laughing.

"Oops," said Sam. The reporter approached again as the shot widened to include all the recent graduates from Bradley who had attended the Bible as Literature class. All of them wore personal protective equipment and stood, grim and determined, like soldiers behind Sam.

"This is Sam Ewing, a civil engineer who lives here in town and recently assisted in some remodeling work done to the school," the reporter said, forcing a bright smile for the camera. "He has some surprising news that may change the fate of this once-doomed institution."

"Yeah, somebody didn't do their homework," Sam growled. "Number one, people are saying the school is too damaged to repair. I inspected the building myself after I heard about this report of it being condemned. The building is completely repairable. I have already filed the results of my inspection with the proper authorities.

"Number two, there's plenty of money to pay for the repairs because the insurance policy we took out on the remodeling job covers any other necessary repairs within the same fiscal year. I don't know who authorized this demolition, but my crew and I are here to put a stop to it right now, and here's my legal authorization to do so."

Sam waved a clipboard with papers to his right as the shot expanded to include the bewildered demolition foreman trying to catch the papers and get a look. The kids all crossed their arms and looked fierce for the camera.

"Mr. Ewing –" the reporter began.

"Sam. Mr. Ewing's my dad."

"Sam, then. What about the cause of the explosion? This station has been told that –"

"Hey!" Sam stuck a greasy-gloved finger in the reporter's face and made her back up again. "News is supposed to be reporting *facts,* not rumors, right? If somebody calls you up and says something, it's gossip until you check it out. Unless you got solid proof of what you're about to say, don't even think about saying it! My business deals in what's true and what isn't, and I thought that's what reporting was supposed to be about, too."

The reporter's eyes got very wide. She didn't say anything.

"I will tell you this," Sam said, putting his hands on his hips. "My preliminary inspection proves that this building isn't unsafe, contrary to what's been reported. My crew and I are going to go over it with a fine-toothed comb, and then there may just be some facts for you to report." The kids nodded in unison on the word *facts*.

"We'd appreciate being kept in the loop about your findings, Mr. –" The reporter dodged his correcting finger again. "I mean, *Sam*. This is Amber Sachs reporting. Back to you, Ted."

Keith, Talia, and Mr. Bradley stood to their feet and clapped.

"That couldn't have been more perfect!" Joshua exclaimed. "Good old Sam."

"I didn't know he was a civil engineer," Talia said.

"Sam owns his own construction business," Mr. Bradley replied. "He was basically volunteering on the crew at the school. He's one of the wealthiest men in town."

"Wasn't he kind of pushing it, though, dressing the kids up and pretending they're part of his work crew?" Keith asked.

"You should know better. Sam would never *pretend* about anything," Joshua said. "I forgot to tell you, didn't I? Brad Shannon called last night while you two were out for a walk. He helped Sam get that paperwork filed. And Sam hired all the kids from the class who were eighteen and over. They are going to be his crew to do the full inspection, and he will do his best to find out the real cause of the explosion and help them salvage anything that can be found from the Bible as Literature class materials."

"And did you see who was on the crew?" Talia ran back the DVR and pointed. "There's Daryl, and there's Sean. They're free!"

"Wow." Keith leaned back in his chair. "I didn't see any way out of this for those kids. I was willing to go to jail myself just to get them out. And I had no idea how I was going to keep the others from snooping around in what I thought was a building ready to collapse."

"God provided Sam to give us a way around that," Mr. Bradley said. "And Dr. Ewing had a part in it, I'm sure. I'm still afraid of that woman."

"Me too," Keith agreed. "The way she talked to me when I called her about Jenny Kaine ... brrr."

"I'm just so relieved that the kids are taken care of, and everybody's safe," Talia said. "So, can we get back to work now?"

"Sounds like a plan," Joshua said, rising to leave the room. "I'm going to work on the Constitutional history site with Cliff Owens. I guess I'll see you two at lunch?"

"Yep," Keith said.

The two of them started organizing and examining material to include on the Restoration site.

"Keith, here's a contact from a teacher who found the Restoration site," Talia said much later in the morning. "Look at what she says, and these images she included. They've found corundum and orichalcum artifacts at Harappa and Mohenjo-Daro!"

"Umm ... where?" Keith echoed. "Wait, someplace in India?"

"They are both ancient cities located in Pakistan," Talia said. "In earlier times it was part of India. Remember the Guardians are still trying to decode the tablets we found in Ugarit. They haven't really been looking elsewhere. But they can't exactly keep the finding of that many tablets a secret. People have been speculating like crazy about a find of ancient artifacts but so far the details have been kept sketchy. This woman has gotten hold of the Britomartis story somehow.

"You know people say that one of the earliest belief systems, wherever they find artifacts, is the worship of a mother goddess. Some secularists claim that Britomartis was a mother goddess. This teacher, though, has a really exciting theory about who mother goddesses might really have been. Come take a look."

Keith slid his chair closer to Talia to read the post. The title said, *Daughters-in-Law of Noah?*

Chapter Fifty-one –Britomartis and Pipali

We know next to nothing about worship practices in Harappa and Mohenjo-Daro, the post said. Still, anthropologists insist that relics point to a mother goddess worship. Some trace the festival of lights in the Hindu religion back to figurines of women that seem to hold lamps. These are tall, slender women with beautiful ornaments and headdresses, not naked fertility figures.

> *"Some scholars dismiss these statues as children's toys and not significant religious objects at all. Suppose, however, that these lights were indeed made for children, as part of the mothers' efforts to teach them the way to faithful protection and sharing of the Word? We also see what some call gods, part-beast male figures, sometimes horned, sometimes with multiple heads. These could be cherubim, something the Scriptures considered common enough that they are barely described, and with varying appearances. It is also possible that they could be evil spirits or demons.*
>
> *"People recognized angelic beings, good ones and evil ones, for what they were in*

Job, in Daniel, and in Ezekiel, just to name a few places. Nowadays our secularist scholars insist these figures are gods. Perhaps the true God sent His heavenly servants as helpers or protectors to the ancient faithful. Men are the first to fall in religious wars. Sometimes their wives simply outlive them.

"Nimrod surely fought against those who opposed his false, man-centered worship. He pursued them to enslave them, or his descendants tried to steal from them or corrupt them. These figures might represent faithful women who had to continue to teach the children or stand against the armies of evil when their men had died.

"I have heard through trusted confidential sources about the discovery of the Ax of Britomartis in Crete. My specific knowledge is scanty, as was my contact's. I hope to gain the trust of those who can fill in the gaps by presenting my theory of a parallel figure in the Indus Valley.

"Another of the ancient representations archaeologists find in the Indus Valley is the Pipal tree. The leaves of the living version of this tree never stop moving, even when there is no wind. Many Scriptures use trees as symbols of being rooted in God, receiving food, shelter, and protection from Him. I see this woman with the lamp as a constant nurturer of others, sharing the Word without ceasing.

"Perhaps you will dismiss my theories as fancy, but please study the enclosed images and consider how they might cause me to connect the woman I have named Pipali with Britomartis. I urge you to consider that these

ancient women might be two of Noah's daughters-in-laws or their descendants. If Noah's sons married much younger women, as tradition suggests, they could have outlived their husbands, possibly by a century or more.

"Pakistan is a dangerous place. I understand if you cannot consider coming here and looking at my findings in person. But please know that the artifacts I have found are real, and that they seem to me to be comparable to ones I have been privileged to glimpse, and which I am told were found in Crete and Ugarit. I eagerly await your response."

"Can we trust this person?" Keith asked.

"She mentions her contact, and it's someone Uncle Naddy and Aunt Sophie have worked with for years. I believe we can trust her. Just look at the artifacts," Talia said, opening the attached image files.

"Whoa," Keith said, his breath leaving his lungs for a second. "That's orichalcum, isn't it?" He stopped himself from reaching out to touch the image of a woman, glittering golden, holding a red crystal bowl in her hands. "And that bowl has to be corundum. What's that black stuff in the bowl?"

"Burned oil, I think," Talia replied. "This is one of the lamp figures. *Thy Word is a lamp unto my feet, and a light unto my path.* This figure is older than anything I've seen from the Indus Valley. Even the female figures she mentioned that I've seen had to be later corruptions of this design. They were called the 'slim' ones, in contrast to those fat fertility goddesses. They were still mostly naked, with lots of jewelry and elaborate headdresses. This one is clothed, and the ornaments are very conservative. The workmanship is superior, too. *Pipali.* I love that name."

"There's a tree figure," Keith said as he touched the screen to expand another thumbnail image. "The detail is incredible. Is that some kind of fruit I can see peeking out from under the leaves?"

"Yes. Pipal trees bear a type of fig. The symbol of Israel has been a fig tree from ancient times. This is an exciting parallel, isn't it? See the tiny marks on every single leaf? Do you realize what those are?"

"They're ... some kind of writing?"

"Exactly. We've got another code. No one knows how to read the Harappan language. But here are symbols all over this tree. And look at the woman's ornaments – the borders on her gown –" she flicked to enlarge the image on the touchscreen.

"More symbols. More code." Keith nodded. "But are we sure this is connected to the Testaments? Those symbols don't look the same at all. Everybody's already scrambling to translate the tablets from Ugarit. We're not even sure Britomartis has a connection to them. That could just be a corruption, like you and Naddy talked about."

"Or maybe this is the connection." Talia pulled up another image. "Look at this carving. It's part of a wall, looks like, and there's one of the male part-animal beings the lady from Pakistan talked about."

"Weird," Keith said. "There's a whole bunch of animals around it, regular ones. But that thing has a bull's body, and a man's head, with horns on it. It looks like a lot of idols I've seen pictures of. What's significant about it?"

"See that man kneeling in the middle of all the animals, with something in his hand, and whatever that is under it? Some people might think he's making a sacrifice and worshiping the part-bull figure, but what if the bull creature is there to protect him, not to be worshiped?

"He almost looks like he might be carving or writing something on that object in front of him. He might be surrounded by animals because he's living in a wild place, or on a farm, away from a city."

"I can see that, now that you point it out. Man, how many textbooks did I read that just assumed all this stuff represented idol worship. I never looked at it the way you described it, or that lady did. It makes so much sense. So the man is writing – maybe like in Ezekiel's vision, God was giving him something to write down?"

"We have to be really careful about how much interpretation we put into these things," Talia cautioned. "The Scriptures say *holy men of old spoke,* or wrote things down, *as they were moved by the Holy Spirit*. So it's not a stretch to say the man could be recording a part of God's Word. He could be making a copy, not something directly inspired. He could be writing down something passed to him orally from earlier records lost because of persecution."

"Right. We don't have enough context to be sure what he's writing. So it's inconclusive. And I still don't see how this connects to Britomartis or to the Testaments."

"Look at this border," Talia said. "On the stonework, just before the broken edge – there." She expanded the image.

"More symbols," Keith grumbled. "Is that Harappan?"

"Yes. But the point is, there are messages here that are worked into the elements of the design. They're hidden in plain sight. Now, let me show you some images from photos the Guardians took at Olous, where we found the ax. Uncle Naddy just received these last night."

She swiped open a new file and brought up underwater pictures. Keith recognized their dive site. Talia expanded a shot at the base of the broken column.

"Somebody's been chipping off the barnacles and stuff," Keith observed.

"Yes. See this border at the bottom of the column?"

"That's orichalcum, not corundum," Keith said. "I see more symbols. Oh, man. We don't just have to decipher the tablets. We're going to have to figure out what all these hidden messages say?"

"Not necessarily. Look what the email that came with these images says."

> *We are beginning to be convinced that in many of these artifacts are repeated copies of similar or identical messages. In other words, structures, clothing, pottery – any kind of man-made object could have been used to make copies of the Word. Small portions, some portable, some wearable, some fixed, but they are simply ways of keeping the Word before people's eyes and in their minds. These cultures wanted to fill everyone's consciousness with as much of the Scriptures as they could.*
>
> *We are not taxed with translating every scrap of these writings. We need only use them for comparison to try to locate and identify the true and complete copies of the Word. There may be more than one set of Testaments, in different languages. The Ugarit tablets may represent only one of the sets."*

"Oh, I get it," Keith said. "Those writings in Olous are copies of parts of the full Testaments in that language that's like Linear A, maybe. But the images we got from that Pakistani lady are a different language, another one we don't know. But they still point to there being tablets, maybe, in that language, somewhere relatively near these artifacts, like the Ugarit tablets were relatively near Olous and Crete."

"Yes. Exactly." Talia hugged him. "No crowds to embarrass us here, right?"

"Right," Keith said, kissing her. "But I wouldn't care if there was a crowd. I love you so much. Are you and Naddy and Sophie planning on having that wedding anytime soon? Because I am so ready."

"Aunt Sophie and I are talking about it," Talia said with a shy smile. "Keith, I think we do need to go to Pakistan and see these artifacts firsthand. I think we can at least hope that there are some more Testaments nearby. But I want to have the wedding before we go."

Chapter Fifty-two – Covert Wedding

“Is the Skype set up?” Keith asked, running into the command center.

“All set,” Bart Matthews said. “Get on into the chapel, Son. They’re ready for you.”

Keith wrestled with his tie as he hurried across the foyer to the chapel. His father caught him in the doorway.

“Let me do that, Son,” he said with a smile.

“Thanks, Dad.” As they walked up toward Pastor Stokes, waiting to officiate, Keith glanced around at the collection of big screen TVs and saw groups start to appear. The Bradley Central gang, other teachers, students, and parents, sat in the school auditorium, waving, grinning, and cheering. Another display showed their friends and pastor in the church sanctuary. A third had Grandma Bradley’s friends from her senior apartments gathered in their community room. Grandma Bradley sat next to that screen, chatting softly on a computer with some of them.

A fourth monitor showed the inside of a tent and Keith could see Jiggly, Cindee, and people he didn’t know who might have been Naddy and Sophie’s archaeology associates, diggers, or even Guardians for all he could tell. Jiggly and Cindee kept waving like idiots and Cindee looked like she was already crying. Keith hadn't remembered her having green hair before. In the background Keith spotted that Israeli pilot, David *somebody,* who worked for Magnum Security and had saved Keith from Jenny Kaine's runaway van. *He looks like he's about ready to cry too. Wow.*

Keith's brother Dan stood beside David and kept poking him and laughing. David, who stood almost a head taller, finally put Dan in a headlock and held him for a full minute. Keith didn't even know for sure where they were, or how Dan had managed to get himself there a week after they announced the wedding date. He didn't know how any of this had come off in such a short time.

"Turn around, Son." Keith did. Sophie entered, wearing a soft blue dress, and came to stand opposite Keith and his dad. Behind her he saw Naddy with Talia on his arm. She wore a simple white cotton dress and carried a bouquet of daisies and buttercups picked that morning from the meadow outside the main building. Her hair was up and stuck full of little white flowers. Keith's grin widened as the people on the TVs went silent. Naddy gave Keith a long, hard look before breaking into a smile and putting Talia's hand into his, patting both of them with his big paws.

"You will never be buried at a dig site," he rumbled as he went to sit by Keith's grandmother.

Keith's cheeks twitched by the time the ceremony ended, he was trying so hard to control his grin. He managed to control the tremors long enough to kiss the bride at the right time.

"I feel like this is a milestone for our Intergrid ministries," Larry said afterwards over punch and cake and thc "congratulations" and other happy screams still periodically erupting from the TVs. Everyone in the remote locations was having something to eat and drink, even the people in the tent. "This is our first covert wedding, isn't it?"

All the residents of the campground looked at each other. "I believe you're right, Pastor," Bart agreed.

"Intergrid?" Keith asked.

"Instead of going off the grid, we've sort of made our own grid within it," Tom Schuster, the man working with Keith's dad on the Constitutional history site, explained. "We have people who do nothing else for us but secure our online communications. Magnum Security does a lot of it. Don't know what we'd do without Drew Summers. He's kind of made us his mission."

"Drew Summers is – what – the owner of Magnum?" Keith's dad asked.

"Yes," Naddy replied. "He was also the owner of the Tesla that is now Talia's."

"He was the guy with the gambling problem?" Keith asked. "The guy who came personally to pick us up from the airport?"

Sophie nodded. "Drew lost everything to gambling. His wife still will not speak to him. He does not even know where she is. Naddy has invested in his business, as have others, since he swore off his Poker addiction. And he helps our cause so much."

"God has blessed him in the two years since he put down his cards," said Eva Sanchez, the woman who managed the campground.

Keith and Talia couldn't help glancing at Naddy.

"Ask no questions for conscience sake," he said with a scowl.

"Okay," Keith said. He took Talia's hand. "So, Mrs. Sanchez, where's the honeymoon suite? You said you wouldn't tell us until after. It's after, and it's almost midnight. Can we –?"

"Oh, of course!" Eva jumped up. "Come. Your chariot awaits."

"Chariot? It's not in this building?" Talia asked.

"I thought you knew everything about this place," Keith said as Eva led them out the side door of the main building.

"It never occurred to me that I would need to know about a honeymoon suite." Talia giggled.

"And we never had one before," Eva said. "Like the pastor said, this is our first wedding here. But we improvised." She waved a hand to show them a golf cart covered in streamers and paper flowers, complete with cans and shoes tied on the back. *Just Married* was written in soap on the clear snap-on side covers. Everyone had come out to shout more congratulations and wave. In the luggage rack sat two suitcases.

"Somebody packed our stuff?" Keith started grinning again.

"Well ... we packed some stuff ..." Eva said with a smile and a wink. "Climb aboard."

She drove down a narrow, packed dirt road into the woods and kept going. The golf cart's headlights didn't show much of what was ahead except more trees. Keith and Talia snuggled in the back of the cart and waited.

The cart broke out of the trees about two miles from the main building and Keith and Talia climbed out, open-mouthed. Near the edge of a clearing where a lake stretched away into the darkness stood a small log cabin. A canoe was tied to the dock. The Tesla sat beside the cabin.

"You stay here for at least a week. Longer if you like," Eva said. "We've stocked it with everything we could imagine you might need. Food, videos, music we were told you liked – there are prepared meals and scratch ingredients, because I know the missus likes to bake. Your choice, what you do and don't do, but come morning, I think you'll see you have some options. Besides ... You know ... the obvious wedding night stuff." She smirked and handed over a set of keys.

Talia hugged her. "Thank you so much!"

"Why are you thanking me?" Eva said, starting to cry. "When I found my husband dead in our back yard, I slit my wrists so I could die too. If your aunt and uncle's colleagues hadn't been stopping in on their way to the states from the Olmec dig, I would have gone to meet God with suicide and hatred on my soul. This place is my peace. And you two are our future."

Keith listened in stunned silence. He had to make himself grab the bags and follow Talia to the cabin as the golf cart drove away. They stood on the tiny porch as Talia fumbled to unlock the door.

"Everybody here has a story, I guess," Keith said, setting the bags inside the door. "What's Mrs. Sanchez's?"

Talia hugged herself and started to tremble. "They ran a mission in their hometown of Ciudad Juarez, Chihuahua. It's a city near El Paso, but in Mexico. They tried to offer alternatives to illegals who thought they had no choice but to smuggle drugs or pay *coyotes* – people who claimed they could get them into America."

"They started the work after finding dead and dying people in their yard or near their house almost every day. Some had drugs inside their bodies in packets that had burst. Some had been cut open to get the drugs. Some, both males and females, had been raped and beaten and didn't even have clothes on. Eva and Raul worked for fifteen years taking people in or giving them decent burials, trying to notify relatives, and sharing Scripture and hope with those who could still hear. Her husband was killed by a Mexican drug cartel."

Keith took Talia in his arms and felt her shaking subside. "I love how she said, 'This place is my peace,'" he said. "So many people have found peace here. Peace, perfect peace. I think I heard your uncle say that a few times. C'mon, Mrs. Bradley." He shifted and picked her up, carrying her inside the cabin.

Talia opened one of the suitcases when they were safely locked in. “Oh!” she exclaimed.

“What?” Keith asked. “Something wrong?” He looked over her shoulder into the bag and grinned. “That must be your bag,” he said, admiring the lacy white object at the top.

Chapter Fifty-three – Rescue by Cab

Talia adjusted her head covering after they had collected their luggage at the international airport in Faisalabad. They waited for more than an hour before Naddy started pacing the floor.

Sophie whispered, "I'm sure our contact told us to wait here. I hope there hasn't been any trouble."

"Hello, and welcome to Pakistan," said a woman in muted robes, approaching them carrying a basket. "Traffic was terrible. I brought you some pipal figs," she added.

"How kind of you," Sophie said. "We have brought precious treasure." Naddy showed the woman small packages Keith knew contained copies of the Scriptures in Urdu, Pakistan's main language. Everyone relaxed after the exchange of passwords.

"Please follow me. We have a taxi waiting."

To their surprise, the woman got into the front seat with the driver after he helped put their bags in the back of the ancient minivan.

"This is my brother," the woman explained. "We have been told that it's best not to exchange names. Your team arrived a few hours ago, and are getting set up at Harappa for us to start tomorrow. I am amazed at how quickly you were able to get permits."

"I am well-acquainted with the antiquities minister," Naddy said. "We have met numerous times in Monte Carlo."

"You have more connections in Monte Carlo than ... than anybody has anyplace," Keith said.

"Connections are what we need as believers," Naddy replied. "After the conversation with your father about purifying my heart, I wanted to swear off gambling. I know the dangers, and the questions that arise about its sinful nature or simply its ruinous possibilities, but now I cannot help seeing it as a harvest field. God did not say stay at the banquet table, even to serve. He said go out. Monte Carlo represents my highways and my hedges as well as my means of funding our work. The Pakistani Minister of Antiquities and I have had many talks. Sometimes people raised in Islam never openly confess that they have accepted the truth. So it is with my friend. But the seed roots itself in his stubborn heart, and he is a gracious host to my archaeological colleagues whenever we have work here."

The taxi threaded its way among buses and tiny cars, as well as donkeys, camels, and wagons. Though the hotel was only a few miles away, it took more than an hour to reach it. The driver and his sister both helped with the baggage, discreetly leaving the packages of Urdu Scriptures in the trunk under a blanket.

"I see what you mean about the traffic," Talia said. She balanced the basket of figs carefully on top of her Doomsday Duffel bag. "Thank you so much for your trouble."

"This is how we live," the taxi driver said. "I will come back to take you to your camp site in two hours, or as soon as I can make my way." He flashed a broad smile.

"Welcome to the International Hotel," a clerk said as they approached the desk.

"This looks like something out of *Casablanca*," Keith murmured to Talia.

"The lobby is beautiful," Talia said. "Let's hope the rooms are as nice."

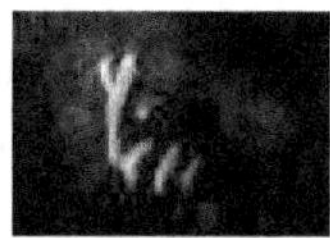

"Yes, yes, we can stay at the dig site if you wish," Naddy said. They had gone into their rooms and Sophie and Talia had come straight back out into the hallway. "All of us. I thought I would ease Keith into the archaeologist life. The hotel should have been better than living in tents."

"Well, this one isn't," Sophie said, crossing her arms. She stared at the peeling paint and wallpaper through the doorway and shuddered as insects of various kinds scuttled freely up and down the walls. "We should have gotten some recommendations."

"Enough," Naddy grumbled. "It has been years since we worked in Pakistan. Back then this was an excellent hotel. I will try to get our money back but I am sure they will just want to exchange for other rooms that are equally ..." He looked up and down the dark, moldering hallway. "I am sure we will not stay here," he said in response to the looks on his wife and niece's faces.

"I'm sorry this happened on my account," Keith said after they had escaped from the clerk and the managers' endless stream of excuses and had piled their bags on the curb to wait for their cab. "I would have been happy to stay in a tent at the dig site in the first place."

"It was strange, how insistent the manager was that we must stay," Sophie said with a grimace. "As if cleaning the room again would make up for rotting floorboards and moldy walls and rusted fixtures. The first time you lay down on that bed, my husband, you would have been into the room below, and in need of a tetanus shot for bedspring punctures."

"It will probably be hours before the cab driver shows up," Talia sighed. "At least these figs are good." She popped one in her mouth.

"They are good," Keith said, taking a handful. "I feel like I'm eating Bible History – Figs are in the Bible a lot, aren't they?"

"Indeed," Naddy replied. "The fig tree teaches of God's blessings of peace and provision. In fact, Habakkuk uses the fig tree to reinforce the lesson that God is the source of joy and rejoicing even when we don't see evidence of physical provision."

All of them jumped as the unmistakable sound of gunfire erupted inside the hotel. Talia grabbed a small case from inside her duffel bag and pushed Keith and Sophie behind a palm tree. She worked frantically to open the case and her gun popped into her hand.

"How did you get that past the airport security?" Keith gasped as Talia pushed Naddy behind the tree as well. It wasn't that big of a tree but they crouched behind the bedraggled hedges as Talia peeked toward the hotel entrance.

"Weapons can go on a plane. They just have to be in checked baggage and safely packaged," Talia said as she loaded the gun. "I asked our trucker friends, Mike and Mary, about their secure box and got one made like it that's portable."

Screams and crashes issued through the front entrance and people began to pour out in various stages of interrupted activity. Kitchen workers, housekeepers, and even guests in various stages of dress ran in every direction.

Look at those windows shattering," Sophie whispered. "That was our floor."

"I'm guessing it was our rooms," Keith said. "Somebody planned on killing us, and maybe bribed the hotel to keep us there? That must be why they kept trying to make us change our minds."

"They should have paid them more, and sooner, to make the rooms habitable." Naddy put a hand on Talia's shoulder. "We have to get away from here."

"Where can we go?" Talia asked. "They'll either know about the dig site and be waiting for us there, or they'll follow us there and kill everybody."

"Who are they?" Sophie asked. "Who would cause all this destruction just to get at us?"

"Jenny Kaine would, in a heartbeat, I bet," Keith replied.

"But before they were just trying to find out what we knew, or steal our artifacts," Talia argued. "Killing us won't get them closer to stopping the work of the Guardians."

"Perhaps they are just venting their anger that we are not there," Sophie said.

They all risked turning around as tires screeched behind them. The old minivan cab pulled up to the curb and their contact opened the front door.

"Get in! Get in!" The brother and sister crouched and shielded themselves as best they could while helping the travelers grab their belongings. The driver tore away as hooded men emerged from the hotel brandishing weapons.

"I can't believe nobody saw us with that pile of stuff right outside the hotel," Keith exclaimed.

"Thank you so much for coming back for us!" Talia said. "How did you know we needed help?"

"We heard on the radio about shooting at the hotel," the woman replied. "We wondered about you going there in the first place, and almost suggested we take you elsewhere. I wish we had. It's a notorious place for tourists to be lured to and taken advantage of."

"Should we take you to your dig site?" her brother asked.

"No," his sister replied before anyone could speak. "The gunmen might follow us. We need to make sure no one can figure out where we take them."

"Then we should take them home," the driver said with a smile.

"Of course!" The woman clapped her hands. "Yes! You shall be our guests tonight."

"We can't endanger you," Naddy protested.

"When you see where we live, you'll understand why you'll be perfectly safe there," the woman assured him. "We live in the Caves of Gondrani."

"Impossible!" Naddy exclaimed.

Chapter Fifty-four – the Caves of Gondrani

"You live in a cave?" Keith asked after the stunned silence stretched on too long. The minivan labored out of Faisalabad.

"No one lives in the Caves of Gondrani," Naddy scoffed. "It is an archaeological site."

"No one has worked the part of the site where we live for years," the cab driver replied. "Many poor people in Pakistan have taken up residence in the old cave dwellings. And so have many who don't wish to be spied upon and threatened."

"So these caves are ... what?" Keith began. "Real caves? In the mountains?"

"They are manmade caves," the woman replied. "No one knows exactly how or when. Some say Buddhist monks carved them out for seclusion. That is convenient for those who do not want to consider the legends of other makers."

"We are not looking for legends," Sophie said. "We need evidence. But ... Are you referring to the tale of Badiul Jamal?"

"The story of Badiul Jumal hints at a deeper truth, perhaps," the woman replied. "A princess haunted by demons, freed by Prince Saif-ul-Muluk, who killed them. This supposedly happened in the time of

Solomon. Arabic legends speak of increased demonic activity during Solomon's reign. The djin or genies are very much like demons, or possibly even angelic beings. The stories say Solomon found a way to imprison the evil djin."

"That sounds like the Arabian Knights – putting them in bottles or lamps or something, right?" Keith ventured. This conversation was starting to remind him of his research into Britomartis. He had thought that was just a crazy myth until he had seen what the ax could do.

"May I ask why you would come all the way to Faisalabad if you live in the caves of Gondrani?" Talia asked. "It's more than a two-hour drive."

"People don't need taxis there. They need them in Faisalabad," the driver said. "I go up once a month or so and stay a week – however long it takes until I earn enough to meet our needs and help some of the others who cannot get work or travel."

"You have perhaps heard about the other story of the caves," the woman said. "The Gondrani people were all tormented by demons that ate their flesh, so the tale goes. A holy woman of great age named Mai freed the people. Some versions say she sacrificed herself. Some say she exorcized the demons and lived out her life in the town. You can visit the shrine to Mai, where she is supposed to be buried, while we are there, if you wish."

Keith could see Talia, Sophie, and Naddy exchanging uncertain looks. Finally Sophie spoke up. Changing the subject seemed like the best thing to lower the discomfort level Keith could feel growing in the taxi.

"How can we let our people at Harappa know we are safe?" Sophie asked. "If you heard about the gunfire at the hotel, they will hear of it also. We don't want anyone to come there looking for us."

"We should be far enough from Faisalabad now that you can try to use your phones without being tracked, if you have signal," the driver replied.

"I cannot get a call through," Naddy complained.

"Yes, but I can text," Talia said, applying her fingers rapidly to the task. "That takes less signal than talk. Okay, there. I got through to Cindee."

Glad 2 know UR OK, the text said when she showed the phone screen around. *Jiggly was about 2 launch a rescue. He's sure gotten a lot braver since he got religion.*

Everyone laughed.

"How far will we be from Harappa at this cave place?" Keith asked.

"Harappa is much closer to Faisalabad," the woman replied. "I'm sorry we had to take you such a long distance out of your route, but we will definitely confuse and throw off any pursuers. It's actually good that things worked out this way. Some of the more important discoveries I have to show you are at Gondrani."

Keith felt Talia tense up beside him. He casually put an arm around her and pulled her close. They sat in the third set of seats, behind Naddy and Sophie. The minivan made a lot of noise and the roads were bumpy, so he risked a whisper in her ear.

"Do you think they're kidnapping us?" he asked. "Maybe working with the crazies at the hotel? They sure showed up at just the right time."

Talia hesitated but finally shook her head. "We are going in the right direction for Gondrani," she replied softly. "I checked my phone GPS."

"If your artifacts are in Gondrani, why did you tell us to set up for a dig at Harappa?" Sophie asked.

"Misdirection for those who might overhear," the woman replied. "And not all the artifacts are at Gondrani. After you see what I have, you will want to confirm and verify that these artifacts are consistent with findings at Harappa."

“So it is your contention that the cave dwellings at Gondrani are much older than the Buddhist theory?” Naddy asked.

“Some of them clearly are. Yes, indeed,” the woman replied. “But I want you to draw your own conclusions.”

“Aren’t the caves dangerous? Crumbling from erosion?” Talia asked.

“Some are, of course,” the woman said. “But we have found those to be mostly the later-period ones. Some cells were made by Buddhist monks, of course. It’s not that people are lying, exactly. It is another case of misdirection. I’m sorry. I’m trying so hard not to influence you. Doctor Ramin –” She nodded her head at Sophie “–said you need evidence, and not legends. So I only ask you to look at the evidence and see what you conclude.”

Just the flight schedule to get to Pakistan had worn Keith out. The terror when the shots rang out at the hotel and the long drive in the taxi left him too bleary-eyed to pay attention to the accommodations. He awoke the next morning with Talia in his arms and an arch of sandy-colored stone over his head.

“Where are we?”

Talia laughed. “Gondrani,” she said.

“Oh, the cave city.” He jumped up and smacked his head on the ceiling. “Ow! Were the people who made this midgets?”

Talia stood up and raised a hand, brushing the cave roof with her fingers. “No,” she said. “They seem to have been more my size.” She slid under his arm. “You said you liked my size.”

“I do like your size. You fit very nicely under there.” Keith kissed the top of her head. “But these places sure weren’t made for people my size.”

"People your size just have to learn to duck," Talia teased. "Come on. Let's not keep our hosts waiting."

"I still can't believe people live in this place all the time," Keith murmured as they met Sophie and Naddy coming out of their own sleeping chamber.

"They have no choice," Sophie said. "Poverty and persecution have dogged the steps of all people who have not submitted to zealots of false religions or secularist persecutors."

"These people deserve our greatest sympathy, but I hope we are not wasting our time here," Naddy grumbled. "How can a taxi driver and his sister have acquired the priceless artifacts we saw in those emails? If this is some sort of deception we could lose more than time. What if we are vulnerable to discovery or attack here?"

A helicopter appeared in the distance. All of them instinctively ducked into an uninhabited cave until they could no long hear the beat of the rotors. Their hosts found them cowering there.

"I wish we could reassure you that you are safe here," the woman said, bringing a waterpot down from her head and setting it on the ground in the cave. Her brother offered towels and fragrant soap. "Please, wash and refresh yourselves, then join us for a meal. After that we will show you what we have here, and you can make arrangements to join your team in Harappa."

After they had eaten, the brother and sister led them toward the edge of the cave city. They passed many "homes" where people waved timidly and children ventured out to smile and stare. Keith saw that their hosts sometimes gave covered baskets to people they passed, and once he saw the corner of an Urdu Bible peeking out.

"So these people really are believers?" Keith whispered. He tried not to let it bother him when quite a few of the villagers began to follow them. He also couldn't help noticing that many of them bore scars and other marks of serious injuries. “They didn’t just decide to live here because they were poor or looking for freedom? They were attacked? Chased out of wherever they used to live?”

“This is the face of persecution,” Talia whispered back. “You’ve seen news reports about attacks on believers but you’ve never seen the results up close. They have lost everything physically, but look at those smiles. They still have the hope of Christ.”

She turned around and started to sing ... strange words, but a tune Keith finally recognized. The whole crowd started to sing along, shouting and clapping. A familiar children’s hymn sung in Urdu was like an anthem of hope. Keith and Talia wiped away tears.

“If you could do genetic testing on some of the people who are here,” their hostess said after everyone had quieted down, “you would learn that their bloodlines are ancient. My brother and I are natives of this area as well. Not all of us were driven here by persecution. Some of us are at home, returning to our true roots. We believe that the people who settled Harappa are all descended from the woman I have named Pipali, and that she was a daughter-in-law of Noah. We in turn are their descendants. People think that the Harappans died out or were subjugated or wiped out by wars. We have a different theory.”

Chapter Fifty-five – The Well of Provision

"Welcome to the Well of Provision," the man said, gesturing toward what looked like a large patch of underbrush. Their crowd of followers began to pull and push at the edges until the visitors realized it was a covering made of woven fibers and dead scrub. When the camouflage was cleared away they looked down into a large well lined with intricate brick designs.

"You may have heard about or seen the great Chand Baori stepwell and others in India," their host said. "But this is much, much older. No matter how severe a drought we have – And Pakistan has had some legendary droughts – this well has never failed."

Keith stared down into the large depression with geometrically-patterned brick steps down the sides, disappearing into the water deep inside. Intricate and beautiful designs covered everything.

"That's incredible," he said. "Did you have to go all the way down there to get us that water?"

"No," the woman said with a smile. "We have catchbasins elsewhere, but that water comes from an underground river. We believe it is part of the lost Saraswati-Ghaggar-Hakra River that once supplied Harappa as well."

"Why have no archaeologists told of finding this place?" Naddy demanded. "We have been warned not to come to Gondrani because of the erosion danger. But someone surely must have reported finding this wonder."

"The secularists who dominate the field of archaeology are unhappy with the very idea of such a find," their host told them. "If anyone has found it they have suppressed the knowledge. Notice that the statuary and symbols do not conform to Hindu or Buddhist styles. They cannot account for the well's origins within the time frames they assign to man's supposed progression from simple hunter-gatherers to complex city-builders. This represents ancient knowledge of techniques we believe were passed directly from Noah to his immediate family and descendants."

"You have no doubt heard people marvel that Harappa contains no obvious temple and no idols," the woman continued. "Such is the case here as well. These people worshiped God in Spirit and in truth. They honored rulers and creatures of God's design, not personifications of demons or men who claimed to be gods."

"Clearly, there are similarities to Harappa in the architecture," Sophie said. "But there are no such statues there."

"That is because they were destroyed by invaders," the man explained. "It was the deliberate intention of the evildoers to blot out all traces of those who worshiped the true God. It is also possible that things were hidden, or that they were moved to safety. The so-called artifacts people display as coming from Harappa were left by the invaders. The fetish idols, so primitive compared to the buildings and other structures, do not belong. They might have belonged to the invaders. But some of us believe they were planted there to tarnish the reputation of the ancient faithful descendants of Pipali."

The brother and sister led them down the stairways into the well. "Take photos, measurements, samples – whatever you need," the woman invited. "But take care who you show them to. People who have tried to share such findings as these end up disgraced or dead."

"We should have our crew here, not at Harappa," Sophie lamented.

"We cannot afford to call so much attention to this place," the man replied. "You must do the best you can with the assistants you have." He spread out his hands to include Keith, Talia, his sister, himself, and the smaller crowd of interested cave-dwellers who had remained with them. Everyone began to descend the steps.

Sophie and Naddy promptly unloaded equipment from their backpacks, and Keith and Talia spent the next few hours holding measuring tapes and scales, using tiny brushes and whisk brooms, and descending deeper and deeper into the step well.

"There is no evidence of radioactivity here," Naddy observed. "No vitrification. How do you account for that?"

"This is the theory we hoped to share with you," the woman said excitedly. "At Harappa and Mohenjo-Daro, you have that evidence of nuclear activity. Skeletons in the streets, fused into the ground. Brickwork vitrified by heat too extreme to be produced by any kiln. Crystallized artifacts. The story is told in corrupted form in the *Mahabharata.*"

"Are you trying to say that the enemies of truth used atomic warfare against the believers?" Naddy asked. For once his excitement was hushed, almost reverent.

"You are close, but mistaken. Let's break for lunch," the brother said. "We'll visit Mai's shrine, and we'll talk some more."

As they ate pipal figs, flatbread, and goat cheese in the shade near the shrine to Mai, the man smiled as Naddy repeated his question.

"No, no, it was not the evil ones who harnessed the power of the atom! Do you not see the similarities in the story of Mai and wonder how she was able to destroy the demons?" The man asked. "What if she was real? There is evidence of radioactivity near here, as if an atomic battle took place. This building people call her shrine, of course, is a much more modern addition.

"Beneath it are ruins, and they have evidence of vitrification. I'm sure you noticed by the water lines that the Well of Provision was at times nearly full in the past. Water can protect against radioactivity. So perhaps the water shielded the step well, and those treasures, from the destruction at Mai's battle.

"What if Mai really lived, and lived much earlier than people have led us to believe? What if she and other Indus Valley dwellers used atomic power against the invaders? We believe that is the kernel of truth in the legends of the *Mahabharata*. Unfortunately, the warfare seems to have devastated their own populations as well. We have done genetic testing all over Pakistan, and the bloodlines we can trace back to Pipali are rare. So few of us remain."

"This is the legacy of those who fight back against corruption," sighed Sophie. "Marauders today are slaughtering believers all across the Levant and Anatolian region. That is only one battleground. Some are fighting back, but believers are called sheep for a reason. Christ was led as a lamb to the slaughter. He opened not His mouth against his murderers. Perhaps some did fight back, but should they have? Was it an act of disobedience?"

They walked back to the step well in silence and Sophie and Naddy resumed their work. Finally their female guide spoke up.

"Christ came to sacrifice Himself. He submitted to the will of the Father. But that does not mean all believers are to dumbly die without trying to protect and preserve themselves and the ancient faith. Better to fight back and lose than commit mass suicide like those at Masada and other places where they had no idea how to stop the enemy," the woman said fiercely.

Keith stopped his dusting with the tiny brush and glanced at Talia. He mouthed the words *Warrior Angel* at her and she fought to control a smile as she stood up and stretched after crouching over a figurine of a tall, slender woman with a bowl in her hands.

"I think we need balance in our attitude toward the wicked," Talia said. "Isaiah acknowledged the pride and idolatry of Moab, but instead of rejoicing over the punishment God promised, he mourned. God may allow us to be an instrument of judgment, but that isn't cause for pride or glorifying destruction. *I have made the shouting to cease. Therefore my heart intones like a harp for Moab and my inward feelings for Kir-hareseth.* God takes no pleasure in the death of the wicked, but desires all to repent."

The woman stared at Talia but didn't respond. After an awkward silence, Talia gestured at the statue she had been cleaning and said, "This is very much like the images you sent us in the email. Just made of clay instead of the orichalcum and corundum materials."

The woman still didn't respond. Keith had to wonder if she'd begun to question putting her trust in them. He could see the uncertainty in the expressions of both the brother and the sister as they exchanged looks. The man took her aside, out of earshot, and they partly talked, partly argued for several minutes. Finally they approached. Naddy, Sophie, Talia, and Keith all stopped what they were doing and waited. The silence started stretching out again.

"We are overwhelmed by your hospitality, your generosity," Talia said. "And the things you have showed us already – All of this is humbling. Thank you so much for trusting us, and for sharing the treasures your people have protected for so long. It can't have been easy to decide to send those emails."

The brother turned his sister to face him, hands on her shoulders. He nodded. She turned back to face the visitors.

"The artifacts from the photos are in the tunnel," the she said at long last.

"Tunnel?" Naddy's ears actually seemed to perk up. Keith was sure of it. "Where is this tunnel?"

"That pavilion down there is the mouth of the tunnel," the man replied, pointing toward the columned structure about halfway down the well. "We wanted you to gain some understanding of the people of Pipali before we took you down there."

"You haven't seen the half of what we have to share," the woman said with a smile. "Come. It's time to show you our contribution to your search for the Testaments."

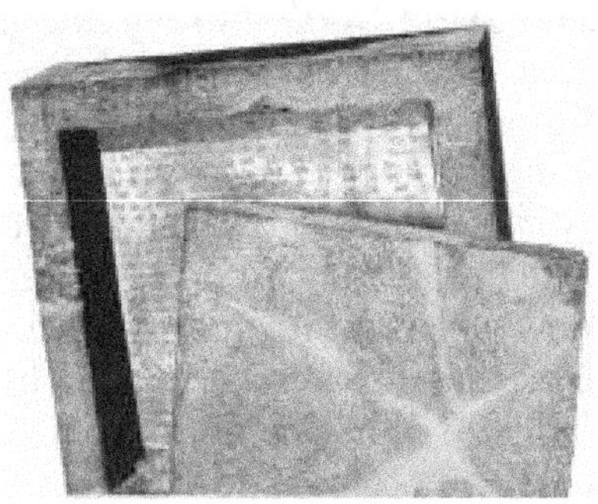

Chapter Fifty-six – Pipali's Library

"I hear running water," Keith said as they entered the cave behind the step well's pavilion. "That must be that river you talked about. Does it go all the way to Harappa?"

"We think it does, but most of the course runs deep under the rocks," the man replied. They held up lanterns and exclaimed over the ornamented doorways leading to side chambers.

"Whenever the temperatures outside grow unbearable, people escape down here," the woman said. "The water makes it a least a few degrees cooler, just like Chand Baori. Poorer people used to sit on the steps close the water, and the nobles had these chambers to rest in."

"Fantastic," Naddy said. His voice echoed. "Fantastic," he said more softly.

"In here," the woman invited, letting them pass ahead of herself and her brother. "We want you to experience this as we did when we first discovered the contents of this chamber."

Keith followed behind Naddy, Sophie, and Talia, but almost ran into them when they stopped dead just inside the doorway of the chamber their guides pointed out. He slid around them to get a look but found himself falling under the spell of a room filled with intricate folding framework stands a little like a sea of camp stools, each one bearing a golden tablet. The stands seemed to be made of ivory or bone and had carvings that reminded Keith of scrimshaw. The part that corresponded to the camp stool's seat was made of the skinlike material they had already encountered. Keith reached out and lifted a tablet. He handed it off to Talia, more interested in the hide holder for the moment.

"This material looks different from the others we've seen," he said. "Have they been kept dry in here?" He looked around as their host and hostess entered. "You said the water in the well gets almost to the top."

"There is a baffle system you might not have noticed as we entered," the man replied. "It prevents the water from entering these inner chambers for the most part. This room, which we call Pipali's Library, has kept almost completely dry, I believe. But isn't the casing material water-resistant?"

"Yeah, it is, but I think the ones we found that had been submerged for so many years ...well ... it looks and feels different. I can see it's the same stuff, but this ... you can see this texture ... was it embossed or stamped or something?"

"We don't believe so," the woman replied. "This patterning is consistent with your theory that it is the skin of an amphibian."

"I was mostly guessing," Keith admitted, "because the water-soaked casings didn't really retain this much texture. Wow. Do you know what kind of creature they made these skins from?"

"We could call it Leviathan, or Behemoth, or even a dragon or dinosaur. Those are just words that conjure images in our minds. They must have been very plentiful, or a few very large specimens. Because the skin on these casings is so very much alike throughout, we lean toward a very large animal."

"How many tablets are here?" Sophie asked, touching a few timidly as if she feared they would crumble under her hands. "We have never seen them firsthand, like Keith and Talia did at Ugarit. This is ... this is a momentous occasion."

Naddy nodded in agreement, apparently speechless for once, Keith noted with a grin. He realized he'd never gotten a very close look at the tablets, either, since they'd hurried so much to gather and deliver the ones they'd found. He took the one he had handed Talia and hefted it.

"How'd we do that, hauling all of those out of the water to the Tesla?" he asked Talia. "These things are *heavy.*"

"I kept thanking God we had the scooters, or we never would have made it," Talia replied. "But there are more here. We can't remove them, of course ..." she trailed off and risked a look at their guides.

"On the contrary, we want you to take them," the woman exclaimed. "They have sat here for centuries, benefiting no one because the language was lost to us. Now at least someone is trying to understand and make use of them. It may be that they will help with understanding the ones you already have, or that those may hold keys to understanding these. Either way, it is clear that they are related."

"How in the world are we going to get them out of here?" Keith asked.

"David Sharon is with the dig team at Harappa," Talia said. "He has one of Drew Summers's helicopters."

"This is a gray area, you know," Naddy grumbled. "We have permits for artifacts from Harappa, and from Mohenjo-Daro, since I thought we might need to cross-reference. But we have no authority to take these tablets out of the country."

"The Well of Provision and the true site of the Shrine of Mai are Harappan – Indus Valley sites," the woman insisted. "Whether they settled at Harappa first, or here, your permits expressly cover related finds determined to also be of Harappan origin, or Daroan. Here. Here are the statues and artifacts I sent you pictures of."

She pulled them into another room and they saw niches containing glittering orichalcum artifacts. "Take them also. We have extra wrappings made of the amphibian skin. They mold into shape and protect the artifacts beautifully. When you get to Harappa, find the great bath and look for the image of Pipali etched into the southern steps. It's very small, hidden under an overhang, and no one else seems to have discovered it.

"But there is a sort of bunker beneath the bath, and you will find more images, and more artifacts. That will make all the connection you need to satisfy the antiquities minister of the commonality of the artifacts. Please, please relight the lamp of Pipali. Teach the ancient truth. Protect it and spread it."

They had to climb to the surface to use the Naddy's satellite headset to reach the camp at Harappa. At first Naddy just kept saying, "What? I cannot understand you. No, I can't make out a word you are saying. What? What?"

"Is the signal that poor?" Sophie asked finally.

"The signal is excellent," Naddy growled. "It is only Jiggly. He has clearly had far too much coffee and is mostly speaking his peculiar brand of hyperactive. Here, Talia, see if you can get him to hand the phone off to someone we can comprehend."

Keith stifled a laugh as Talia verbally wrestled with Jiggly. Keith was sure she was speaking Italian at one point but the words came out so fast he wasn't sure.

"Oh, you're already on your way with David?" she finally asked. "Why didn't you say so? You have our location, right? We'll see you in about an hour then. No, I can't really tell you what we found over the phone. You'll see soon enough. Yes, you can hang up now. Good-bye, Jiggly."

"This stuff is like stretch-wrap," Keith exclaimed. "It sticks where you want it to and lets loose just as easily. I've got to get some tests done on these new skins."

They hustled to get as much packaged as they could before the helicopter's arrival. The amphibian skin in its un-waterlogged state was a marvel. It formed itself around the artifacts and tablets. Volunteers from the cave settlers had been of enormous help and the children stared wide-eyed at the candy bars Keith and Talia offered them. Keith snapped pictures with his phone as they tasted the chocolate.

"This is their first time, ever, right?" he said softly.

"To eat chocolate? Looks like it," Talia said with a smile.

"I think I hear the helicopter," their male guide said. "Keep working. I'll go and show them where to land."

The workers had to keep splashing themselves from the well every time they carted loads of tablets out into the full sunlight. The bricks had heated up and sweat poured off Keith as he dragged another armload out and looked up.

"Shouldn't the helicopter have landed by now?" he asked as Talia joined him, panting, and they passed their tablets off to the bucket-brigade of volunteers moving the precious cargo up to the top of the well.

"Oh ..." Talia stared up at the shadowy craft as it passed over the well. "I thought David was going to bring a different one. That one looks awfully small."

"We heard a helicopter when we got up this morning," Keith recalled. "What if that's somebody else ... somebody trying to find us or spy on us?"

"Keith, our hosts said we're safe here. That must be David. Come on. We have to keep moving. Obviously we'll have to make several trips to Harappa."

Before long Jiggly came clattering down the steps and almost landed in the well. Keith dragged him back just in time.

"Look at all this stuff!" Jiggly exclaimed. "More tablets? The Guardian guys will go nuts!"

"Let's just hurry up and get them out," Keith said.

"Come on, Jiggly. Give us a hand," Talia said.

"Well, I was going to say I cut my finger almost to the bone, but, no, The Warrior Angel speaks, and what can poor Jiggly do but obey?" Jiggly sighed, and started back up the steps with a load.

Chapter Fifty-seven – The Honor Is to Serve

Keith looked up and saw David Sharon's towering silhouette at the edge of the well. He waved at them and started down. Jiggly spluttered and got red in the face when David met him on a narrow ledge and kept him weaving and bobbing in a minute-long dance before he let him go by with a laugh and a slap on the back.

"Shalom, Evangel and her heart-holder," David said as he accepted loads of tablets from both Naddy and Sophie. Keith felt a twinge of envy as the Israeli pilot's muscles bunched up under his black T-shirt. He had almost twice the tablet load Keith could hope to carry out. "And to you as well, Doctors Ramin. The honor is to serve." He bowed his head and took the steps double-time.

"So that's what they mean by hinds' feet on high places, right?" Keith said. Talia looked up at David.

"He works out all the time," she said. "Hours every day. He used to say he had to sweat away the black thoughts. But he's so cheerful and sweet, I can't imagine what black thoughts he could ever have had."

"Talia," Naddy said, "and Keith, we are almost done here. Perhaps this is as good a time as any to share David Sharon's history with you. You may need to know at some point how we met him."

"Naw, I know how it is. I bet you met him at Monte Carlo," Keith joked.

"Wait ... I remember now, that he said he owes you and Aunt Sophie," Talia said. "Uncle Naddy, how does he even *know* you? I just played wargames online with him, and covered for him sometimes when he skipped out of required login times. Did he say he owes you because you got him the job at Magnum?"

Naddy pulled them both aside into one of the chambers for royals inside the tunnel. "I met David Sharon before he went to work for Magnum. Possibly you knew him earlier through his online persona, Talia, but the night I met David Sharon, he was in an Israeli prison, accused of butchering a whole family of Palestinians with a combat knife as they slept in their beds."

Talia covered her mouth and turned white. Keith just stared blankly at Naddy.

"What?" he said. *"What?"*

"David's parents were both teachers at a school he attended as a boy– that is, his father was headmaster, just as your father is at your school, Keith. His brothers and sisters attended classes there as well. They were a large family – seven children. He was fourteen years old when he became the only survivor in his family from a RPG attack on the school. As the years went by he made no secret of his various plots to find and kill the man who attacked the school.

"In the meantime he enlisted and became a stellar airman, highly decorated and extremely well-known, though not by the name of David Sharon. If I told you his real name, Talia, I am sure you would remember his feats. Perhaps even you would know him by reputation, Keith.

"But all along the way, bitterness filled his heart. Israelis live with death every day from Palestinian attacks, and so many have lost loved ones and live fatalistic lives. But he used to say his rage sparked the flame of his life of conquest and victory. All this he told me in the prison cell on a night when the government contemplated publicly executing him to appease those participating in the latest futile round of peace talks."

"Executing him?" Talia breathed.

"Yes, and the prospect pleased him," "Naddy said. "He said his grief would finally end, and he would be remembered as being the Avenger of Blood for his family. But a friend who knew David's family extracted a promise that I would help him. He had proofs that David was not guilty. The man who was murdered was indeed the one who had fired on David's school. The Palestinians freely acknowledged it.

"But the executions were done by Palestinians who knew about David's blood-grudge and planted evidence of his guilt to remove him as a threat. When I laid before him the proofs that my friend had gathered, he pleaded with me to destroy them and walk away.

"I had made a promise. My friend was a high-ranking official who could not afford to become publicly involved. I, on the other hand, had nothing to lose by turning over the proofs to the Israeli government. I owed my friend a debt and this was his choice for how to settle it, by saving David's life.

"David, however, believed ending his life would end the agony of the loss of his family, a wound he had reopened every day with his schemes for vengeance. I told him no such thing would occur. He would have eternal memory. Peace would never be his. I do not know why he believed me. But he did, and you never saw such a strong man, such a courageous one, crumble and weep as he did. I left him in the cell weeping, and hurried to present my proofs to the prison official.

"He looked over the evidence. Then he looked up at me, got up from his desk, and hurried me back to David's cell. He unlocked it and waved us away.

"'Take him,' the prison official said. 'Get him out of here. Out of the country. Now. Tonight. I will wait to make this public tomorrow, when the repercussions cannot touch him. Go. Now.'

"So I dragged my young friend out of there, no small job, since he could not see his way for tears, and chartered a private jet. Someone smoothed the way through what is normally the strictest security in the world, and we left Tel Aviv at three am, David a free man in body but with no concept of what to do with all those years of bitterness, grief, and rage, when he was reprieved but left with no life or identity.

"He was an empty shell for many days. Sophie and I sometimes had to practically feed him, dress him, make him get out of bed each day. Finally my friend who had secured the proofs of his innocence managed to leave Israel secretly and came to see him. I had not known until the day he came to the tiny apartment we had rented for David that he was Messianic."

"Yeah, David said he was going to turn Dan into a Messianic, but I'm not real sure what that means. A Jewish Christian?" Keith asked.

"There are many kinds of Messianics, but, yes, in David's case, I know it means accepting Jesus Christ as Messiah," Talia said. "They often struggle with how the Scriptures, the Law, and all the Jewish traditions, apply to them. I know David struggles with it."

"My friend counseled him to accept Christ, and we believed he did," Naddy said. "But the blackness he runs from still mars his peace. He blames himself for the death of innocents in that Palestinian man's family. He still grieves for his family. He misses Israel, his comrades in arms, the thrill of flying fighter missions and helping to protect his homeland.

"He still feels lost and rootless. He tries to trust Christ, and prays all the while that he punishes his body with exercise. Working for Magnum has distracted him somewhat, and he seems better these days. Something may have happened to push back the blackness."

"What was that?" Keith asked as the ground shook. They ran out of the tunnel to the pavilion. Rocks rained down from the edges of the well and clouds of smoke and dust rose to blot out the sky. "Something exploded?"

"Look! That's Magnum's four-seater, still on the ground! But where did that other copter come from?" Talia cried. "What is he doing? Shooting! He's shooting at the people!"

"David is taking off. He's trying to shield them with his helicopter!" Keith shouted. "What can we do? We have to help these people!"

"Amu and *Zanamu*, you two get back into the royal chambers." She started pushing her aunt and uncle into the tunnel. "Get far inside, and stay there until we come back for you." Keith and Talia shoved them in the right direction, with all the villagers who were still below with them.

Talia pulled out her gun as they ran back to the tunnel entrance. She fired up toward the unmarked, sand-colored helicopter as people ran screaming from it and the larger Magnum craft swung around to run interference. The shots made the attacking copter veer away.

"Follow me up, Keith," Talia ordered. "Come on!" She started running up the stairs, still pausing to shoot, and Keith kept as close as he could. They hugged the wall and though the attackers tried to shoot at them the shots just made dust clouds along the wall. Finally the tan helicopter took off away over the desert, just about the time they reached the mouth of the well.

"Get in the helicopter, Keith," Talia shouted as David touched down again. None of the villagers were in sight and only the sound of the rotors disturbed the eerie quiet. Keith could see David frantically waving.

"Wait, we have to get Naddy and Sophie up," Keith said. "And you're coming too. We're all coming. Where's Jiggly? Did Cindee come?"

"Please don't argue. I'll go get *Amu* and *Zanamu,* but I need you to go ahead."

"No way I'm leaving without you," Keith said. "Everybody comes or nobody."

"Keith, David won't leave unless there's another threat. But he knows the mission is to protect the tablets and to protect you. Please don't argue. This is too important."

"What are you talking about? Protect *me?* We have to protect *everybody.*"

"You're needed to help with figuring out the technology to share the tablets. You're the only one who's made any headway. You're the priority, along with the tablets."

"No. No way! There's nothing special about me. And even if there was, you're my wife. You can't think I'd leave without you. And Naddy and Sophie ... no way I'd leave them behind."

Keith saw Talia's expression change and turned around just in time to see David get out of the helicopter and head toward them. Once he ducked to avoid the rotors, he advanced toward them so rapidly Keith hardly had time to react.

"He is not picking me up and carrying me into that helicopter."

"Only if you force him. I love you. I'm going down to get the others. Please go, Keith."

Talia scrambled away down the steps. David came to a stop in front of Keith, his eyes deliberately staying on Talia's retreating figure and not meeting Keith's.

"We will have a problem if you take off before they get up here," Keith said to David.

"More problems than you can imagine," David said with a slight bow.

"No, I mean between you and me," Keith retorted.

"Understood," David replied. "But for now, I suggest you don't make this any harder than it already is."

"Fair enough." Keith followed David back and got in the passenger side of the copter. "You really can carry everybody and all these tablets too? And get us out of here in a hurry?"

"Yes. That's why I chose this copter. Magnum has no craft with a better payload-to-speed ratio."

"What about the villagers? Can't we use this time to help them?"

"They best know how to protect themselves," David replied. "The villagers are not the target and I've been checking – as far as I can tell, they are all safely undercover now." He put on his headset and pointing at a rack over Keith's head. "There's one there for you, as well, and we can communicate with those below via the satellite phone."

Keith sat with his fists clenched, staring at the lip of the well. A group came up, including Sophie, Cindee, and several villagers. The villagers scattered and vanished before the women even made it to the helicopter. Sophie and Cindee joined them inside. Keith knew it was no time to confirm his wedding-day suspicion that Cindee's hair was a strange shade of sea-green, but he couldn't help it.

"Naddy's having a hard time making it up," Cindee said. "Talia and Jiggly are both trying to help him but his face is so red. We're afraid he might be having a heart attack or something."

"Evangel, can I drop a harness for your *amu*?" David said into his headset.

"Yes, we should try that," Talia's voice came back in Keith's ears.

"Let me get out and go help them," Keith said through gritted teeth.

David shook his head. "Strap in," he announced, and lifted off before Keith could even get a hand on the door. The helicopter swung out over the well and a door in the floor opened. David deployed a cable and harness as he maneuvered into a position where they could see Talia, Naddy, and Jiggly struggling up a flight of steps. Naddy grasped the steps above him, bent over and huffing.

"What I need you to do, Heart-holder," David said, "is to hook yourself up to that safety harness against the wall on the opposite side from me, to try to keep the craft balanced. You need to be ready to pull Dr. Ramin in when he gets up to the opening. The cable will operate best if you don't touch it. Just make sure he doesn't get hung up at any point. Understood?"

"Sure." Keith hurried to take his position and snapped the harness around himself. The copter adjusted, corrected, and overall moved far too slowly for Keith's taste. Finally they hung immediately over the side of the well where Talia and Jiggly seemed to be using all their strength just to keep Naddy from sliding off. His face had gone from red to pasty and Keith struggled mentally with Talia as she wrestled the harness into place around him, while Jiggly pushed and pulled Naddy in the right directions.

"All right. Take him," Talia's voice gasped into the headset. David's hands moved fluidly and the copter swung Naddy free of the ledge. He hung in the harness like a dead weight and Keith heard Sophie start to sob. The winch reeled the cable slowly upward. Keith spared a glance at Talia and Jiggly as they started to climb the steps.

Jiggly jerked upright and toppled over the edge. A puff of dust hit the wall next to Talia. She still tried to grab at Jiggly but his body leaned outward and fell, hitting several banks of steps as it crashed down into the well. Cindee and Sophie started screaming.

Keith could see the desert-colored helicopter rise into view as more shots pinged around Talia and their craft. Naddy started to spin crazily and Keith had to grab his body to steady it and guide the path of the cable into the body of the copter. Out of the corner of his eye he saw David unlimber some kind of machine gun from a rack behind his seat, slide his door slightly open, and unleash a volley at the other copter, forcing it to retreat out of range.

The Magnum craft bucked and twisted before David left off shooting and righted it. Keith, Cindee, and Sophie got Naddy buckled into a seat. The women got an oxygen mask and started to work on Naddy. When Keith turned around to deploy the harness again, he saw that David had shut the bay doors.

"Open the doors back up! Drop the harness for Talia!" Keith screamed at David.

"Can't ... sorry ... something jammed the doors. I think some shots hit them. Heart-holder ... I need your help up here."

That was when Keith saw the blood. He lunged forward and caught sight of David's upper arm, sleeve and flesh shredded.

"First aid kit ... under there." David had wedged the joystick between one knee and his other foot and he indicated a small compartment with his toe. Keith dug out the kit and bandaged David's arm. All the while he kept an eye on Talia as she climbed toward the well rim. Steps had been damaged by the shots from the attacker and she slipped and grabbed for a purchase more than once.

"No!" Keith cried out as the pale helicopter swung back into view and started peppering the ledge. David grabbed up his gun, cracked the door, and started firing at the attacker again. The Magnum helicopter wobbled and Keith tried to help him steady it.

"We're too loaded down for me to maneuver like this." David let a curse slip through his teeth as he reached back to secure his weapon with his injured arm. "Sorry. Sorry. I'm going to try to set down."

"What are they doing?" Keith saw the belly of the other copter disgorge an object.

"It's some kind of weapon!" Cindee screamed. "Oh my God! They're bombing the well!"

David jerked the controls and the Magnum copter shot into the air, swinging over sideways and twisting them all in their harnesses. Keith hadn't had a chance to strap in, still trying to finish bandaging David's wound, and he was flung down against the winch in the floor headfirst. Stars shot through his vision but he managed to see, upside down, through the bottom of the Plexiglas door, Talia launch herself off the cliff, feet first, toward the pool at the bottom of the well, just before the other helicopter vanished and blast went off.

Chapter Fifty-eight – Static in the Headset

"Mr. Bradley ... Keith ... Please, can you wake up? David can't fly the copter. Please, we need help!"

Keith opened his eyes and stared up at Cindee tugging his shirt almost off of him, trying to lift him out of the recess where he lay tangled up in the rescue harness. His head pounded but he saw David hanging halfway out of the pilot seat and felt the helicopter dipping and weaving crazily.

A weird crackling sound made him remember that he still had the headset on. He assumed it had been damaged when he fell, but had no time to worry about it. Lurching forward, he applied more gauze to David's wound and bound some cloth Cindee shoved at him around it as tightly as he dared. David's eyes fluttered open and he raised a hand to tap the ear piece on his headset.

"Yeah, I guess it's broken," Keith grunted. "Keeps making those noises. How do I level this thing out? Hey! David! C'mon, the copter is – like – flying drunk, or something."

The two of them fought with the controls for several minutes. David's voice was barely above a whisper but Keith managed to follow his instructions from the co-pilot seat, which appeared to have duplicate controls. He was tempted several times to rip the headset off to stop that annoying click-pop-static sound. David could barely move but he continued to twitch his head and fiddle with the earpiece.

"Okay, so where do we head now?"

"There's a hospital not too far from the Harappa site," Cindee supplied. "We already had to take Jiggly there because he almost cut his finger off. Oh, my God ... Jiggly." She sobbed into her hands, trying to muffle the sound.

David nodded and together he and Keith got the course set. David sagged back in his seat and whispered, *"Alive,"* fixing his eyes on Keith.

Keith glared at him. "There is no way." He was fighting tears so hard. That image of Talia sailing off the cliff feet first wouldn't stop repeating in his mind, eyes open or eyes shut. "Can I take this stupid headset off? It won't shut up with that – y'know – crackling and stuff."

"Alive." David tapped his ear piece. "Morse code. *A-L-I-V-E."*

"You mean that's *Talia?"*

David nodded.

"Of course, Talia of many languages would know Morse Code." Keith wanted to hug David. "How do we make this thing go faster?"

David smiled and pointed out the throttle. "I'll tell Evangel you're coming," he whispered.

"David will be fine," Cindee reported as Keith prowled by the ER doors with two cans of AMP and she joined him in the waiting area. She grabbed one and had it open and half gone before Keith could ask if she wanted it. "They had to give him some blood but most of the time it was just nurses admiring his six pack. I didn't think they were allowed to have lustful thoughts here.

"Naddy ... not so sure." Cindee sighed deeply. "He did have a massive heart attack, and they have a surgeon coming to operate, but they complimented us on getting him here so fast and said there's hope. He's as comfortable as they can make him, and so is Sophie, in a recliner by his bed."

Keith didn't want to remember that insane helicopter flight with David passing in and out of consciousness and his headset full of not-so-helpful hospital personnel trying to help him land on the roof, demanding patient vitals for Naddy, and filling his ears up far worse than the long-out-of-range Morse Code scratching that he longed to be able to hear again.

"So how can I get back to the caves?" Keith demanded.

"You can't. Look at the news." She pointed to a grainy broadcast showing black and brown clouds billowing up over a scrub-filled landscape.

"Is that Gondrani?" Keith sank into a chair. All the voiceover and captioning was in ... *Urdu? ... whatever ...*

"They're saying drought conditions collapsed more of the caves and somehow a brushfire got started," Cindee grunted. "No, I don't speak Urdu, or much of anything they speak here, but it's all anybody that speaks English is talking about here in the hospital. Some people are even complaining about squatters being careless with campfires. Somebody sure had a cover story ready."

"Nobody said anything about the bomb, or the shooting? Nobody here saw that David was shot?"

"The bullets passed in and out, I guess. They didn't find any in him. I ... I didn't want any trouble, or too much attention, so I just didn't offer any explanation. They don't even know we came from Gondrani and not Harappa."

"Yeah. I guess that's best. Those poor people living in the caves," Keith murmured. "But ... I have to get back there. I have to find Talia. Just because she's alive doesn't mean she isn't hurt. She needs help."

"I know. I know. Look, in half an hour or so, Dr. Tariq Hamza, the local liaison who's helping us with this dig, will be here. Sophie's a mess, so I have to stick around and help her reassure him that ... I'm not sure what we can reassure him of, but I need to be here to do that. Afterwards, we'll get over to the Harappa camp and I can get the Land Rover. I know how bad you need to get to Gondrani, and I'm with you, but it's the best I can do."

Keith nodded, drank AMP, and started pacing again, rubbing the back of his neck. "What about the tablets and stuff in the helicopter?"

"They've promised no one will touch the helicopter until David can fly it out of here. That reminds me. He showed me how to lock it up. We need to go do that before Dr. Hamza gets here."

Keith and Cindee made their way up to the roof. Cindee secured all the doors to the helicopter and Keith noticed that the keychain had both a Star of David and a cross hanging from it.

"David's something else, isn't he?" Cindee murmured as she fingered the ornaments on the chain. "He wanted me to stay, but sometimes you don't have to understand the language to grasp the meaning. I couldn't take those nurses clucking like hens over a new rooster, even in Urdu, or whatever. He was so embarrassed."

"Yeah, he is something." Keith tried to ignore the wrench in his gut, watching Cindee's transparent worship of David. He wanted to do a little worshiping of Talia, but at this point, he didn't know if he'd even hear clicking in the headset. *Alive. Just keep believing it. She's alive.*

"Wow, that hen and rooster thing – it doesn't sound like archaeologist talk," Keith laughed.

"I grew up on a farm," Cindee replied. "Becoming an archaeology assistant was my way of escaping. Not so glamorous, after all. I still spend most of my time in the dirt. It's just older dirt."

"Well, at least you have a sense of humor about it."

"Keith, don't you wonder who sent that helicopter? And the gunmen at the hotel? Do you think it was that reporter who tried to kidnap you? We never had trouble like this on digs before. Everybody says how special you are, and you're the key to figuring this Testament stuff out. So, since they couldn't kidnap you, are they just going try to kill all of us and snuff you out too?"

"I wish I could say you're crazy for thinking that. Jenny Kaine could be behind all this, yeah, but she's just one reporter. She already tried to track us or make us sick by our Bibles. And she did that exposé to discredit believers. It failed pretty miserably. Now she's shooting at people and blowing up ancient archaeological sites? She must be crazy."

They went back downstairs and checked on Sophie and Naddy. Keith thought his color and breathing were better. Sophie looked very worn and worried, but said the surgeon had informed the staff of his arrival time and any minute they would come to prep Naddy for surgery.

"Find our Talia, Keith," Sophie said. "Continue the work. Don't be afraid of what men can do. What God can do is more. So much more."

"Sophie, Dr. Hamza will be here in a few minutes. I figured I could help you –"

"I will deal with Tariq," Sophie said, pushing them toward the door. "Go. Get the Rover. Find our Talia."

They caught an elevator and when the door opened David stood inside, grinning at them in spite of looking pale and just a little unsteady on his feet. His T-shirt looked a lot worse for the wear, and Keith could see a little of what the hens had been clucking about.

"What are you doing?" Cindee gasped. "Did they release you?"

"Here are the signed forms acknowledging it is against medical advice and absolving them of blame if I drop dead." David waved a sheaf of papers. "I'm taking you in the helicopter to Harappa to get the Rover. The life of the flesh is in the blood, remember? I just needed a little more life, and now I'm good to go. Besides, you need a lecture about leaving me in the clutches of women I care nothing about, my Luna Moth."

Cindee turned scarlet. Keith covered his mouth with his hand and still snorted out a laugh. David swung an arm around Cindee and kissed her as soon as the elevator doors were shut. Then it was Keith's turn to blush.

"Are you sure you're okay to fly? Because I am not that great with the co-piloting stuff, as I'm sure you noticed."

"I've been teaching Cindee," David replied. "She's all but licensed. She was just freaked out because of everything that happened. You can regather your strength for the task ahead in the back seat, Heart-holder. My Luna will catch us up on her beautiful wings if we start to fall."

Chapter Fifty-nine – The Big Bathtub

They made it safely away from the hospital to the dig site at Harappa. Keith could hardly focus on the ancient city as the helicopter passed over it, but he had to ask one question, to be faithful to the people at Gondrani who had sacrificed their safety, their heritage, and maybe their lives, for the cause. "Where's this big bathtub?"

"You mean the great bath?" Cindee pointed and snickered. "Never heard it called a big bathtub before."

"The lady at Gondrani said we'd find more artifacts under there," Keith said.

"First we must find a way to get back to Gondrani and into that well," David said.

"I've been checking the news on my phone," Cindee said. "I'll drive us anywhere, but they're saying the caves are off limits. Seismologists even recorded something they thought was a minor earthquake, which might have been the explosion, or might have been something the bomb disturbed. Look at these satellite images, Keith. You can see the fires all around the well site, and it looks more like an ash crater than a step well. Whoever bombed it knew what he was doing."

"So maybe Talia made it into that tunnel where they had the chambers for the rich people," Keith said. "Those tunnels have to go somewhere. Are there any maps?"

He got out his own phone and started searching while David landed the helicopter. "There's some information in here about an ancient river ... Yeah, the one they mentioned, with the big, long name."

"Saraswati-Ghaggar-Hakra," Cindee said.

"Okay, right. That one. The lady said she thought that river was deep underground, running under Harappa and Gondrani. We could hear it under the tunnel in the well down there."

"It's so *far*, though," Cindee said. "Even if we find out the well and the great bath are connected, it's not like there's a road, or even a clear path. How would we get through? And we could be in an upper cave level while Talia's trapped down below somewhere. I'm sorry. I'm sorry, Keith. I wish I knew what to do."

"We can take a look under the great bath," David said. "It can't hurt."

"So many people have worked at Harappa. You really think there's something they haven't found?" Cindee said. She shut up when she saw the look on Keith's face. "Sure. Okay. Come on."

They changed clothes and instructed the dig supervisor to store the tablets and artifacts from Gondrani. Keith had to settle for some of David's clothes since all of his were still at Gondrani.

They grabbed some packs of food and medical supplies from the camp and made their way into the city with Cindee casting anxious glances at David. "Are you sure you're up to this?" she asked him. "Shouldn't you eat something, or rest, or ...?"

"My Luna," David said softly, "when Evangel can eat and rest, so will I. You know how I am about paying debts. Perhaps, at long last, I can pay this one I have owed the Doctors Ramin for such a long time."

"Okay." Cindee still kept sneaking looks at him as they moved on.

Keith couldn't imagine how David could keep going. *God keep us all going, and Talia too.*

"I though a great bath would be ... bigger," Keith said as they started walking around the brick structure toward the southeast end. "I mean, I've heard about those Roman baths, and how big they were ..."

"Maybe the difference is that the Romans were self-worshipers," Cindee said, "and these people, from what we've been learning, were serving the true God. I've read that this might have been used only in religious ceremonies. What if it was a baptismal pool?"

"What if it was a place of healing, like the Pool of Bethesda?" David asked.

Keith and Cindee stared at him.

"Jesus healed a man at Bethesda," Keith said cautiously, "but that whole thing about the angel stirring up the pool... people say that isn't in there, really ..."

"So I've heard," David replied. "And it doesn't matter whether there was an angel, or it only happened *at a certain season,* or how healing might have taken place beyond the miracle Yeshua performed. Of course He healed that man. It was not the pool or the place. Yeshua showed that the power to heal came from the Father and not a physical place or thing. Still, people would not have brought their sick there if its reputation was completely a myth.

"That man would not have kept lying there, praying, trying to get to the water, if no healing had ever taken place. The Jews at that time were not fundamentally superstitious or even spiritually believing people who expected angels or miracles. The Sadducees who ruled over them believed in no miracle, no spiritual reality, just as most Jews do today. Yet people came to Bethesda. They came, they waited, they hoped. Paul the apostle said, *The Jews seek after a sign.* Why? Because something, sometime, had happened there. *Someone* was healed."

"Yeah," Keith agreed. "Maybe this was the Harappans' place of worship. Maybe it was a place where lots of spiritually-powerful events took place. Why not? We tend to get scared when people talk about miracles, but they do happen, and a lot of them happen in water. Jesus told the blind man to wash in the pool of Siloam. Elisha told Naaman to dip seven times in the Jordan."

Cindee stepped down to the ledge that ran around the base of the steps going down into the bath. A fair amount of water stood in the bath from a recent rain. It was clean, and she knelt down and scooped up a handful.

"Lord, please heal David's arm," she said, "so I don't worry about him anymore. Thanks." She poured the water on David's bandage, almost playfully. He flinched, but only a little.

Keith tried to busy himself looking for the Pipali image, not wanting to see a disappointment over this belief in a magic pool. But he found himself praying all the same.

God, I could use a demonstration of Your power, myself. I want to believe you'll save and protect my Talia, heal her if she needs it, and I know she must need healing, so, yeah, please, heal David's arm. Please. Help my faith, because I need to believe in miracles if I'm going to believe my wife is okay.

"The one thing they kept harping on at the hospital was not to get it wet, Luna," grumbled David. "Now I have to change the bandage." He started slowly unwrapping the gauze. "Or, maybe I don't."

Keith saw a flash of white as David tossed the bandage at Cindee and she screamed. *Man, she is a screamer.* Keith turned around and saw that David's arm had no sign of injury. He didn't look the least bit pale or unsteady anymore, either. Cindee grabbed his hand and stared at his arm in disbelief. He folded it around her and kissed the top of her head.

"Oh, I see the Pipali drawing," David said, pointing over Cindee's head. "Right down there."

Keith and Cindee followed his lead as he squatted and pointed out the petroglyph. Keith put his fingers into the design and traced along its edges.

"Hey, come on, this is an archaeological site," Cindee complained. She started digging in her bag. "We have to use gloves and brushes and be really careful not to compound the deterioration."

"We have to find Evangel," David said, grunting as he pushed against the bricks. "The woman said there was a chamber under here?"

"Yeah." Keith joined him in exploring with his fingers, and after a moment something scraped and slid and the stairs moved aside, revealing another set beneath them. "Which one of us did that? What did we push? We have to be able to do this again."

After another hour of pushing they had figured out where the mechanism that opened the chamber lay. Down into the dimness they went, Cindee cracking what Keith thought must be industrial strength glow sticks. The first thing they did was to find the interior mechanism that would let them back out. Once that was accomplished, they explored the chamber and quickly fetched up against objects in skin cases.

"We need to look at these," Cindee murmured. "But before you say anything more about Talia, yes, later. Look, there's another Pipali pictograph. You guys with the magic touch, start looking for another Open Sesame way down to the river, if there is a way. I want to sneak a look at these artifacts, since we kinda got interrupted at Gondrani."

David and Keith moved around the chamber after failing to find anything near the Pipali drawing.

"This is just a storage room," Cindee commented finally. "I'm guessing the Harappans kept things they needed for the original ceremonies down here.

"On the other hand, we've concluded that the objects related to the tablets are different from the ancient civilizations' artifacts. They're all later works, since the Guardian craftsmen were looking to preserve copies of the whole Scriptures, early in New Testament times. This does look like Harappan writing on some of these, though. Why would they use a language that was already lost? How could they even do that?"

"Maybe it got lost later," Keith suggested. "Maybe they knew it all the way up to those times, but persecution kinda wiped out everyone who knew it after that."

"Or, it could be like some of the Guardians are saying, that they were never languages, but some kind of code based on symbols, pointing to a need for a key," Cindee added. "Now that we have artifacts like the Pipali statues, we might get keys from them. Maybe we're ignoring something about the artifacts we already have, like Britomartis's ax."

"This is not helping us get down to the river," David said. "I know this Golden Testament quest is important. Drew drilled it into my head before he agreed to hire me, that the mission was what mattered, but right now, all I can think about finding Evangel. There are no writings, no symbols, nothing on these walls besides that one petroglyph. If there was just some clue about how to get below this room ..."

Chapter Sixty – Where Go the Boats?

Keith went back to staring at the Pipali etching. "Okay, the statues they had at Gondrani just had her standing, holding that light in her hands, or it was sitting at her feet. But the one up by the steps – it had the light as part of her headdress, right?"

"Yes," Cindee agreed.

"And this one ... It's got the light behind her ..." Keith squatted and stared some more. "Any chance the different positions of the lights could be clues to a direction? Say the one up there ... the light is on her head because we had to go down, below the sunlight, to get in here. So if this one has the light behind her, maybe the passageway we're looking for is in the floor. If I was lying on my face, the light would be behind me."

Cindee and David joined Keith on the floor. Cindee handed out whisk brooms and glow sticks and they dusted and crept around. They moved the artifacts several times.

"Here!" Cindee crowed. All three of them dug and pulled at a ring set into the floor. It was attached to a smoothly-fitted square stone. David pushed them aside and pulled on the ring with all his strength. His veins stood out and sweat covered him, but the stone didn't budge.

"Wait – stop!" Keith exclaimed. "I don't think it's a matter of strength." He rubbed at the stone and found faint images carved into it. Pipali's slender figure was repeated three times. She faced different directions and extended a hand outward.

"They're damaged," Cindee muttered. "I don't see any kind of lamp."

"Yeah, but think about it," Keith said. "This was probably some kind of escape hatch. Anybody had to be able to get it open, or at least an ordinary person in a big hurry – not – you know, just somebody like him." He jerked a shoulder in David's direction. Cindee and David smiled.

"You're right," Cindee agreed. "There's got to be another directional cue, or something else that makes it easier."

Keith tried twisting the ring in different directions. The base did move by quarter-turns, clicking as it went. The clockwise direction seemed to offer much more resistance so he switched to counter-clockwise. After moving three clicks, he felt the base catch and the ring sank slightly. He tried clockwise, and this time it moved freely six clicks before the base dropped again. The ring was hard to grasp now. Keith's fingers were too big to fit.

"Let me," Cindee said. She slid her pinkie into the ring and maneuvered it counter-clockwise. Two clicks, and the base popped upward, along with the stone, lifting the whole assembly. David grabbed it and set it aside. All of them could hear rushing water below. They looked down into blackness. Even Cindee's glow sticks didn't give them a view.

"Here." David produced a long, high-powered flashlight from a belt clip and shined it down. "It's the river, all right," he reported. "But it's twenty feet down. If there's a boat dock, or any way down, I don't see it."

"Probably whatever they had was made of wood, and disintegrated a couple of centuries ago," Cindee sighed. "It even flows in the general direction of Gondrani. So Talia can never get to us this way. We have to get to her somehow."

"We just need to get a boat down there," Keith insisted.

"How?" David asked. "That opening is less that two feet square."

"These people who lived here used this somehow," Keith said. "We can use it somehow."

"They used it when the river was twenty feet higher up, or out in the open," David retorted.

Keith lurched to his feet and stared around the small room again. They had searched it down to the dust in the corners, for clues of any kind, but they hadn't searched for ...

"Look," he said. "Here are some of those frameworks that look like ivory, just like the ones from Gondrani. But they're just stacked, not set up." He grabbed one and pulled it into 'camp-stool' position.

"No room to set them up here." Cindee shrugged. "So what about them?"

Keith set the statue on the stack and fiddled with the frame and skin holder. He twisted it different ways until it snapped out of the camp stool mode into an L shape. He grabbed a second one, flipped it into the L shape, and set them flush against each other.

"They've got extra pegs and holes, and they snap together in different shapes," David marveled, grabbing more frames. Cindee scrambled to get the artifacts and stack them out of the way as the two men rapidly connected frames until they had something about the size and shape of a coffin laid out on the floor.

"The skin stuff sticks together really well. Maybe it's watertight." Keith smoothed and pinched edges together. "Okay, this will still fit through the hole, right? Do we have any rope?"

Cindee nodded and pulled a coil from one of the supply sacks. Keith tied one end of the rope to the ring in the stone and the other end to the edge of a frame at one end of the improvised boat. David and Keith wrestled their creation through the hole and carefully let it drop down to the water. The current immediately tugged it downstream until the rope ran out.

David aimed his flashlight downward and they watched anxiously. "I can't see for sure how much water it took on when we dropped it in," he reported, "but it's staying buoyant. We need to make one with a prow. Keep watching it to see if it lists or starts sinking, Luna."

He and Keith quickly assembled another craft, this time more deliberately boat-shaped.

"Outriggers, maybe?" Keith suggested.

"Yes, and we can make two hulls and fasten them together below," David agreed. They quickly finished assembling the new structures to the point where they were ready to go down the hole.

"Won't we need paddles or poles?" Cindee asked. They looked around the room again.

"Nothing comes to mind," Keith said. "We need to see, and we need to avoid obstacles somehow. That current looks kind of fast."

David grabbed three or four more frames, took them completely apart, and then snapped just the ivory-like shafts together. He was able to make two poles about twice the length of his arms, covering the ends to the middle with layers of skins wrapped thicker at the ends, somewhat like kayak paddles. "These should be some use to push off the walls or other obstacles, or maybe paddle if we have to. Any other flashlights, Cindee?"

"No, sorry. Lots of glow-sticks." She dumped them out of a bag.

"Thread them around the top of the framework," Keith said. "It's something. Oh, yeah. The skin material tears with the grain," he recalled. "We'll need lashing material to tie the parts together."

"I guess this is a bad time to say I get seasick," Cindee muttered as she tore strips of skin and the two men finished the boat parts.

David embraced her. "I do too," he confessed. "And airsick, in a fighter jet, no less. One time my flight crew gave me a case of barf bags. They swore it wasn't a *gag* gift, but, really it was, you know. Come on."

Keith and David ended up releasing their first experimental rectangle of skin and frames because they couldn't control its awkward shape. They grunted and strained to get the outrigger and double hull parts down without losing them to the current. Lashing the parts together was exhausting and unending torture. David's face was green from more than the glow sticks. They hadn't even let Cindee come down yet, trying to spare her the worst of the rocking and dipping and almost-tipping-over episodes.

"Okay, Luna," David called out in a ridiculously cheerful voice, considering they were both battered, beat, and he had just heaved over the side three times in rapid succession. "You're going to have to jump. Make sure your rope is secure under your arms."

Cindee tossed down their supply packs first. The men caught and stowed them. After that, she didn't even seem to hesitate. She jumped in, clear of the boats, and David fished her out and hauled her in beside them.

"Welcome aboard the *Luna*," David laughed, untying Cindee's rope. He pulled out a combat knife and held it against the second one anchoring their boat to the ring up inside the storage room. "Anchors aweigh, Captain?"

"Yeah," Keith said nervously. "I guess it's time to answer the question, 'Where go the boats?'"

Chapter Sixty-one –Air Pockets and Flotsam

How long it was before Talia experienced something besides numb limbs and bone-shattering pain, she didn't know. Between hitting the water *so far below* and the buffeting from the explosion, she had no power to do anything but float and try to find an air pocket. But she had to keep shoving her shoulder against her head, smacking against the satellite headset, beating out the rhythm in Morse Code, *A-L-I-V-E*. It was rated waterproof but she doubted it would last long through all this.

The rain of rocks and dirt kept defeating her quest for something to breathe. She would undulate and flip her body, dolphin-like, limbs useless, toward a weak shaft of light, find a spot to gulp a single mouthful of air, and then choke and reel against mud and grit, bang her head against some unseen object a few times, and wobble off in search of another gulp of air.

More flailing and twisting, another precious air bubble ... *gasp ... gulp ... choke, bang-bang-bang ...*

"Move on or die." The voice repeating in her head almost sounded like the Israeli female drill instructor she had trained under a few years back. Had that

phrase been part of the training? She didn't remember it, but it made sense. *Move on or die.*

Just as the rain of rocks seemed to slow, something new started agitating the water and pulling at her body. The numbness was fading a little, but oxygen was necessary to get her limbs working and it was a bigger problem to get than before, now that it was clear she was being pulled downward, away from where air was most likely to be found. A whirlpool sucked her in circles. She remembered assuring Keith she had been trained to hold her breath a long time. *How long? Long enough, with nothing stored up? Not likely.*

She tried to fight the pull but it was useless. Down and to the side she went, spinning, spinning. Her lungs burned and strained and the numbness was starting to creep back. One final hard whack of her whole body against a rock wall and she sucked in, unable to resist. Water filled her with cold, gritty silt, and a sense of doom.

Something bumped against her, a floating thing, and she grabbed onto it to pull herself upward. Finally she found air. Now she just had to cough out all the water and garbage she'd inhaled and breathing would again be possible. Her head felt like another explosion had gone off before this process had progressed far enough that breathing did her any good. She lay half-in-half-out of the soup-thick, silt-saturated water on a rock ledge, still clutching whatever had allowed her to drag herself back to life.

"Oh, *God.*" Jiggly's arm lay in her death-grip. He had somehow snagged on a spar of rock made jagged by the explosion, and they both lay on what was left of the beautiful pavilion at the opening of the tunnel. Talia made her hand release the limp arm and she scuttled back from Jiggly. Her joints protested and she collapsed again, content to just breathe for a few moments.

Something made her take another look at Jiggly. She could see a little red running from his shoulder wound. *Do dead people bleed?* She couldn't remember. Her legs and arms still alternated between rubbery paralysis and spastic jerking. She had heard nothing for the longest time, and prayed the deafness was temporary, from the shock of the explosion. So when she finally got back up next to Jiggly, all she could do was lay her head on his chest to see if he breathed. No vibrations. No rise and fall. *But his eyes are shut. Aren't dead people's eyes always open, except in movies?*

Another movie scenario popped into her head. Somebody comically waking up from near death and worrying or complaining about being kissed. *Kissed.* Mouth-to-mouth. *Jiggly. Can I? Is there any chance he's ...?*

"God, I need help, if I'm going to give Jiggly mouth-to-mouth. I need ... I need You to make me do it, and I need it to work."

Talia was saying the words out loud, but couldn't hear them, and wondered if she was whispering or shouting. Then she wondered why it would matter. *Help me.* She flexed more numbness out of herself and got into a crouch. Her fingers wouldn't cup or pinch or do anything right at first. *It's been too long. He's dead. He was dead when he fell off the cliff. Look at the bruises ... the broken places ... Why are you even trying?*

"I haven't got enough faith to believe God can bring you back from the dead, Jiggly," she said to the unresponsive form after she finally managed to get the first set of breaths into him. "But I think you saved my life, so I need to try to save yours."

No more doing chest compressions, the EMTs say. They said it does more harm than good. Thank God. I have no strength for that. None. She pushed more breaths in, watching Jiggly's skinny chest inflate.

And that was when the volley of muddy water shot out of his mouth and almost went down her throat.

"Ooohh!" She pushed his head over to the side and he convulsed and curled up into a ball, making horrible faces. One of his arms didn't seem to work at all, the one with the shoulder wound, and he jerked when he landed on that side. Talia pulled him over in the other direction but it wasn't as if there was any comfortable spot on the broken-up pavilion. A thought occurred to her and she staggered drunkenly up on her feet and into the tunnel.

The room from which they had taken the tablets stood almost undisturbed. They had only taken a couple of the frames along as examples, and the rest, plus a small pile of extra amphibian skins, lay on shelves. Talia grabbed an armload, no small task with her slowly-recovering ability to actually make her body obey her. She made her best possible speed back to Jiggly and tried to pad the rocks beneath him. She could tell he was in severe pain, even without being able to hear him.

She searched her sodden backpack, a scaled-down version of the Doomsday Duffel bag. She found her first aid supplies, double-bagged in plastic. The outer bag had shredded but most of the things inside were still dry. She shoved pain medicine into Jiggly's mouth along with a swallow from the only bottle of water that hadn't burst. He choked again but she tipped and massaged and got him to swallow. She poured as much disinfectant into the bullet hole as she dared and padded the shoulder wound with all the gauze she had.

He curled up again and she sagged back. She wanted to shove all the rest of the pills down her own throat, just to stop the muscle cramps and jolts of pain. She didn't even try to examine herself for broken bones, assuming since she could walk and use her hands the feelings were mostly shock and maybe some torn ligaments. She knew she had to stay alert to help Jiggly until help came for them both. *If it was coming.*

The satellite headset was gone, apparently sucked away by the whirlpool. So was her cell phone.

After a while she stumbled to the edge of the shattered pavilion and looked up. Stunned, she stared at the crazed boulders and sheets of rock leaning against each other, almost covering the mouth of the well. No helicopter could come down that way. Not even a climber. It could collapse at any time.

"I have to move Jiggly back, farther inside. I have to do it *now.*" Tremors shook her, and it took her a full minutes to realize it wasn't more muscle weakness. *Earthquake.* She crouched and dragged at the skins under Jiggly's body. Finally he started moving, spasms indicating how much she must be hurting him. But she had no choice. The collapsing rocks fascinated her as they fell downward, making no sound. But dragging Jiggly took too much concentration. At long last she rounded the corner into the tablet room and stopped dragging Jiggly. Consciousness fled.

Later, after a hazy period of sleeping and possibly fainting, Talia made Jiggly swallow some more water, sipped some herself, and shared a tube of peanut butter with him, or tried. Aimlessly she wandered farther back into the tunnel, and almost fell into the yawning cavern where it ended, with a rushing river disappearing below the jagged edge.

"This ... wasn't here before," she commented, and shocked herself by being somewhat able to hear the words. She stared down at the chasm. *How far down is that water? Too far. But where does it go? The wrong way,* she had to conclude, watching it foam and froth and disappear under the rocks beneath her feet. She sat down. The name *Saraswati-Ghaggar-Hakra* started rolling around in her head, a cross between a song and a chant, matching the rhythm of the water. “Even if the river ran the right way, I haven’t got a stick of wood, much less a raft or a boat. Somebody smarter than me will have to figure out how Jiggly and I can get out of here.”

She kept staring at the water and rolling *Saraswati-Ghaggar-Hakra* around inside her head. After awhile she got up and checked Jiggly. He had a fever and shuddered at her touch. She slid the water bottle between his lips and he jerked and made her spill the rest of it.

She stared at the puddle of water as it disappeared into Jiggly’s matted, filthy shirt. “Keith is smarter than me, right, Lord?” she asked. It was good to hear her own voice again. It was starting to sound close to normal. She wished she could hear Jiggly’s annoying voice, too, but so far he hadn’t said anything.

Keith. “He’s going to come for me. When I was tapping *Alive,* I heard somebody tap back, *Coming,* before I lost the phone, didn’t I? Didn’t I, Lord? Oh, please tell me someone’s coming.” *Please.*

She dug in her pack, pulled out her paracord and the little grappling hook, tied the bottle’s neck securely, and spent a long time dangling it down into the water, gradually filling and spilling and filling again, until she had most of a bottle. She bathed Jiggly’s face and head, dropped a purifying tablet in, and made him drink. The game of filling and using the water kept her occupied for some time. She tried to apply more antiseptic to Jiggly’s shoulder and to ignore the angry swelling. Neither she nor Jiggly had kept their watches. The light that seemed to penetrate the rockslide that had once been a well was too uniformly gray to give her an idea of whether it was night or day.

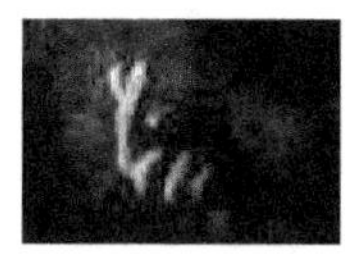

A thudding sound woke her one of the times she slept beside Jiggly. She spun around, firing up all the hurts again. Now it was pitch dark. She snapped a glow stick, hung it around her neck, but had to creep to get back toward the river's edge. Looking down, then holding the glow stick at arm's length. she saw a strange thing butting up against the rocks. Some kind of big, long, box ... a frame ... something that looked like the amphibian skins stretched over the sides. It sagged. It was half-full of water.

"What is that? Where did it come from?" *And why?*

She got her paracord and hook and played *Go Fish* until she caught the corner of the frame. Fighting to drag the thing up when she had no real strength was ... *challenging*. By resting it on outcroppings and twisting to drain water from it, she finally pulled it up to her level.

"This is made of ... it's the frame pieces from those tablet stands ..." Talia stupidly snapped and unsnapped the pieces. "Who would have thought of this?"

Coming. Keith! Talia snapped together two poles, surprised at the strength of the delicate-looking framework pieces. She wrapped pieces of skin around them and made the travois she'd thought about ... *how many hours ago?* Dragging it back to the doorway of the tablet room, she said, "We have to get ready, Jiggly. Help is coming. *Keith* is coming."

Chapter Sixty-two – "Anywhere You Need to Go"

"God, thank You so much for healing David, because we would be dead so many times if he wasn't here, doing this," Keith breathed as David slammed out with his pole and deflected the boat away from another rock wall. They spun in the middle of the river. Cindee bailed frantically with a skin pail, because they always shipped half a boatload of water when that happened. Keith paddled fiercely with his pole while David complemented him on the other side, and the boat righted itself and continued on down.

The oversized baton flashlight was like a pencil beam in the darkness. They usually only had a moment's warning before a wall flashed up almost in their faces. But their crazy craft seemed almost indestructible. Keith had to wonder how far they would have to go, and whether they would find Talia at all. When they had explored the tunnel in the well, he had not heard or seen any sign of the river beyond that one brief sound of its rushing.

Unless something had changed, there was no way they would find anything but more tunnel. Keith could feel everyone's exhaustion. *What a stupid plan. All we wanted to do was find Talia, but how can we do that, God? How can we hope to do that?*

"Heads up!" David shouted, and rammed his pole forward again.

"Whoa!" Keith and Cindee lurched forward as the boat took a nosedive and threatened to slip under a rock shelf. David threw his arms up and caught a rough spot in the cliff face. Keith levered himself onto a two-inch ledge below him. Cindee grabbed a pole and jammed it between two out-thrust surfaces. The boat scudded and shipped more water, but it held. David groaned and Keith grunted while Cindee bailed enough water out to keep the boat from being pulled under by its own weight. The side clattered harmlessly against the rock wall when the pole popped loose. David groaned again.

"If we drop down, the boat's going under, isn't it?" he asked.

"Yeah, I think so," Keith replied, his face smashed into David's leg. "Cindee, can you jam the pole back in there?"

"It's too wet," she said, crying. "It just keeps slipping out."

Keith could only see with one eye, but he wondered about the strange gray light above them. Something tickled his shoulder. *Cave. Spider!* He jerked and almost lost his footing. David grabbed his shirt with one hand, still clinging to the rock by one set of fingertips.

"Steady, Heart-holder," he said, quite calmly. Keith scrabbled and his feet held. David grabbed his other finger holds again.

"What's that?" Cindee asked. "On your shoulder, Keith."

Keith twisted. A blue paracord seemed to have tangled itself in his collar. A paracord with an itty-bitty grappling hook.

"Keith. You came." Keith stared upward and saw Talia's battered face and matted hair above him.

"Evangel." David just breathed the name out. "Is that cord secure?"

"I've been tying knots in it for ... I don't know how long ... the frame pole is anchored against a doorway ... *yes ...*"

David grabbed the cord and scrambled up. Keith wanted to scramble up too but he had to wait for David to drop the cord down again, and he was nowhere near as good at rock climbing as David, so it ended with the pilot hauling him up and rope burns under the arms. None of the last few hours' pain and exhaustion mattered as much once he got Talia in his arms again.

He was barely aware of David getting Cindee and the boat up. All of them lay there, in a state of collapse, until Keith could make himself move a few inches and start checking Talia out.

"You look awful," he whispered.

"I know I must," Talia said with a weak smile. "But Jiggly looks worse. We have to get him out of here."

"Jiggly?" Everyone echoed her. For the first time Keith saw the travois leaning against the tunnel wall. They all gathered around, staring in awe at Jiggly's sagging form.

"We still have some medical supplies left, right?" David asked, Cindee. She went back for their packs. David knelt and sucked in a breath as he examined Jiggly's wound. "Evangel, you're a very bad nurse."

"I know, I *know,*" Talia murmured. Keith hugged her but she winced and he eased up. "We're just alive. That's all. I didn't have the strength to do anything else. I'm sorry."

"He's going septic," David said. "I don't know why he's alive."

"I tried to pray for a miracle," Talia whimpered. "I just didn't have enough faith." She burst into tears against Keith's already-soaked shirt.

"Hey, c'mon, please, Talia," Keith said. "Nobody's blaming you."

"Is this water from the river?" Cindee asked, handing David a pack and holding up Talia's water bottle with the other hand.

"Yes. I used up my water purification tablets. But I tried to cool his fever. I *tried* ..."

Cindee embraced Talia and kissed her bruised cheek. "Shhh, sweetie," she said. "We're going to help Jiggly now. Keith, maybe you should let Talia give you the tour of the improvements, post-explosion and earthquake, to the tunnel. Maybe the two of you can also figure out our exit strategy together, now that you're not distracted with worry."

Keith supported Talia as they made their way to the mouth of the tunnel. He stared up at the crazy rock puzzle. They sat down on the unbroken part of the ledge.

"*Amu* and *Zanamu*?" she asked in a little thin voice.

"Sophie's okay. They were getting ready to do surgery on Naddy when we left. We've been out of touch awhile." Keith pulled out his phone and dialed the hospital. "Yes, I'm calling to check on Dr. Nader Ramin, please? Um ... I'm his nephew-in-law, I guess ..."

Talia smiled and took the phone. She spoke Urdu, Keith had no doubt. Her voice got stronger as she talked. When she hung up, her smile was stronger, too.

"Critical but stable," she said. "*Zanamu* says the surgeon is optimistic. Thank you for leaving to take care of him, Keith."

"It wasn't just him," Keith admitted. "David got shot up. We had to go. We just had time to hear that *alive* of yours." He pulled her close, very gently.

"And to say *coming?*" Talia nuzzled against his neck. "I didn't dream it?"

"No. No dream. David said he told you, since I don't speak Morse Code, either."

"David was shot? Was he hurt badly?"

"It was a flesh wound in his arm, but, wow, it bled a *lot*."

"He was climbing the rock ... he seemed so well ... how?"

"Oh, Cindee tossed some water from the great bath at Harappa on him and asked God to heal him so she wouldn't have to worry. Did you know they're ... a thing?"

"A thing? Cindee and David? What kind of a thing? But ... wait ... Cindee prayed, and God healed him? Healed him completely? Right then?"

"Yeah. My faith wasn't big enough, for sure. I had no idea it would happen."

Talia started to cry. Keith held her and didn't say anything for awhile.

"It's not your fault, or anybody's fault, about Naddy, or Jiggly," Keith said finally. "About whether they live or die. How many lepers were there in Israel? How many blind? How many demon-possessed, paralytics, dead people ... whatever? Did Jesus heal them all, even when He was there with them every day? One time, I think the Scriptures say, *He healed them all*. But that was probably just all the ones there that day, that time.

"The apostles probably healed more people than Jesus did. Some people get healed. Some people laid by that pool at Bethesda all their lives and never got up and walked. God is God. When a miracle happens – when somebody gets healed, it's for one reason. It glorifies God. Maybe it glorified God that David was able to do all he did to help us get here to you, so that's why he got healed. Maybe there's nothing more Naddy or Jiggly have to do to glorify Him. Talia, my sweet Talia, we trust God. That's all we do. When *nothing* goes right, we trust Him."

"Cindee said we were supposed to be figuring out a way out of here," Talia said after another silence. "Did you do it yet? Because I didn't figure out anything."

"Yeah ... no. Neither did I. We need to, huh? For Jiggly's sake." They got up slowly, Keith supporting Talia again. It worried him, how fragile she seemed, but he didn't want to say so. *Something's not right with her*. They needed to get out for her sake, too.

"Hello! Is someone down here?" a man's voice called.

Keith and Talia turned. Talia gasped and held her side, almost falling. Keith scooped her up in his arms.

The taxi driver who had brought them from Faisalabad stepped out of the room where the tablets had been. "You're still here? the helicopter had left, so we thought everyone was safely away. Come. Oh, dear, the young lady doesn't look well. There is a passageway to the surface through here. Come. I can take you anywhere you need to go in my taxi. Anywhere."

Chapter Sixty-three – The Care Coordinator

The man carried one end of the travois-turned stretcher. David carried the other, with Jiggly not even making a sound. Keith tried to carry Talia, but she came to herself and insisted on walking with Keith and Cindee's help. The trip out was rough, and they stared in horror at the devastation. Many more caves had collapsed. The surrounding area still smoked above the acres of charred brush. The taxi driver's sister joined them and they all rode back to Harappa. David prepared the helicopter to fly Keith, Jiggly, Talia, and Cindee to the hospital.

"I'm so sorry about what happened to your people," Keith said to the brother and sister just before they boarded the helicopter.

"You got all the tablets?" the sister asked.

"Yeah. We did," Keith replied.

"Then the message is safe," she said. "That is the most important thing. God's hands hold us up and cover us. Everything else is about protecting the Word. Thank you."

"Your wife has internal bleeding," a doctor told Keith through a woman interpreter. "We can't be sure of the extent of the injuries without surgery. But in the meantime she gravely neglected and overexerted herself. Where have you been, and what in the world happened to her?"

Keith opened his mouth but nothing came out. The interpreter pulled the doctor aside and spoke rapidly to him. doctor's expression softened. He turned back to Keith and the interpreter relayed his next words with a sympathetic smile.

"I am hopeful, since she is in such excellent physical condition," the doctor continued. "We still must do surgery as soon as possible." Keith hurriedly signed forms.

The interpreter reached up and patted Keith's shoulder as the doctor turned and walked off. "She is in good hands. We'll keep you informed."

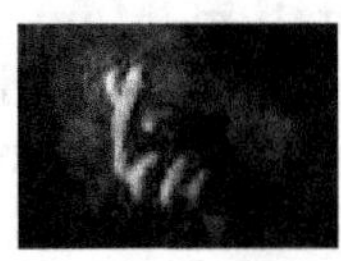

"Hey, Dad," Keith said as he collapsed in the surgery waiting room and grabbed his buzzing phone. "I was just about to call you. Wow. So much has happened, I don't know where to start."

"Let me start, then, Son," Joshua Bradley said. "I called to explain a picture I just sent you. Did you get it yet?"

Keith checked and stared at a plastic freezer bag. It contained a fair quantity of what looked like grayish-white powder.

"Dad, what is that? Are you crazy, sending me a picture like that? What if somebody saw it, and thinks you're a terrorist spreading Anthrax or something?"

"They can't think anything worse of me than I already think of myself. You don't know what that is, do you? It's what's left of your grandfather's Bible."

"What? That can't be. How do you know?"

"Your grandmother called for help at two in the morning," Principal Bradley responded. "She can't sleep through the night, as you know, and sometimes gets up and reads one or the other of the Bibles she has – hers or my father's. She keeps one on each nightstand. She reached over while turning on the light and found this pile of dust there."

Miraculously, Keith had been able to recover their baggage intact from Gondrani. "But we all have our Bibles. At least, I think we all do. They're perfectly fine."

"Yes. So is your grandmother's and so are all the ones here at the camp," Joshua agreed. "We've been checking with our online contacts. Nobody else has mentioned anything like this happening to any other Bible."

"Are you positive this is Grampa's Bible?" Keith demanded.

"As positive as your grandmother is. You're the scientist. Explain it."

"I guess ... Grampa's Bible had to be fifty or sixty years old, right? He would never change to a new one. Just kept taping up the old one. So the scanning process – that little trace of radiation we found – did this because the Bible was so old, maybe?"

"I suppose that's possible," Joshua shrugged. "How many people have a Bible as old as his was? Even my mother's only using the one she got at his funeral. That one's no more than ten years old. So maybe it'll be all right. I guess I might have overreacted. I'm sorry. You said you had news about your trip? You've only been there a couple of days, haven't you? Did you already find something?"

"We found something, all right ... more of the tablets, and some artifacts that may have clues about how to decode the tablets. Not really sure yet, what they're going to do with all these tablets in languages nobody knows."

"That must be discouraging," his dad said. "But at least you are finding things."

"Yeah ... wow, it really has been only a couple of days, hasn't it? The price tag's getting kind of high, though." Keith sighed, then launched into as succinct an account as he could of all that had happened. Silence greeted him on the other end of the phone. "Dad? Are you still there?"

"Son, I can't tell you how sorry I am," his father said. "Here I got all worked up over that Bible ... So maybe Naddy will be all right, in time? But you don't know about this Jiggly fellow? And Talia? She's ...?"

"Still in surgery," Keith said. "Yeah, I don't know anything much. I haven't even checked up on Naddy's condition. I was sitting here, trying to figure out when the last time I slept was ..."

"Keith, you have to get some rest. I can't believe you went through all that. But you'll be no good to Talia if you don't sleep. I remember how bad it was when your mother got sick, and some of those times with Joana – You have got to take care of yourself, Son. I just can't believe you're able to get good medical care right there in the country. How is that possible?"

"Yeah, I was worried too, let me tell you. But people on Naddy's dig told me that a couple of years back, some medical group decided, with all the archaeologists and tourists – can you believe Pakistan *has* tourism? – Anyway, they decided that they ought to take advantage of what they call *medical tourism* in Pakistan.

"People want to find cheaper ways to get medical care, so they go to other countries. Besides that, they just want good care when they are traveling and have an emergency. So they built this state of the art facility, just outside of Harappa, and it was only finished last year. It's amazing. Aside from most of the people speaking Urdu, and the nurses wearing head coverings, it's like being in the states. Thank God it's here."

"I agree, we need to be very thankful. Can you tell me more about this healing you mentioned?"

David and Cindee appeared and stood back by the waiting room doorway.

"I will, Dad. I'll send you text or an email, later. But I might be getting some news right now, so I'll call you back when I know more." He hung up the phone. David and Cindee came the rest of the way in and sat down with him.

"How's Naddy? And is there any news about Jiggly?" Keith asked.

"Something weird's happening, Keith," Cindee said, hesitating before speaking. "All of a sudden they're saying Naddy, Jiggly, and Talia's cases are being taken over. We heard something about a care coordinator. Poor Sophie. They took her away from Naddy's recovery room and kind of herded us all together in a conference room. They said they won't be able to give us any information until the care coordinator doctor arrives. But they sure asked us a bunch of questions."

"It felt like an interrogation," David said. "But before long they realized Cindee and I are not relatives, and not even listed as responsible parties for anybody, so they told us we had to leave. Before all this, it seemed like they were willing to talk to any of us, and it was just care issues. Now, they want to know how the injuries occurred, our locations ... they want to know too much, it seems to me."

"So you think someone's figured out something about the real reason we're here?" Keith asked. "Well, I'm a responsible party, and maybe I can do something to help Sophie, plus learn what this is all about."

David and Cindee guided him to the conference room they had been ejected from and Keith flagged down someone traversing the hall. That person, unfortunately, spoke no language any of them could manage to communicate in. He left but returned with the interpreter Keith had spoken to the doctor through.

"Mr. Bradley, I was instructed to find you. Why did you leave the surgical waiting room?" Her manner was far less warm than before. Caution, even suspicion, clouded her expression. "Please come with me."

She pulled him into the conference room. Sophie sat huddled at the end of the table. The rest of it was filled with people who stared at her with open hostility.

"Please excuse the interruption," the interpreter said, keeping her head down and gesturing for Keith to sit across from her next to Sophie. He sat and sneaked a hand under the table to catch hold of Sophie's. She barely reacted.

"Doctor Ramin has been avoiding our questions," the man at the far end of the table said. "Perhaps now we can get some answers. You are Mr. Bradley, the science expert on this expedition? You are the husband of the injured woman, Natalia Ramin Bradley?"

Keith forced himself not to react to the accusation that Sophie would dodge questions. "Yes, I'm Keith Bradley. I'm not sure expedition is the right word for what we came here to do. I'm just a high school science teacher. My wife teaches Literature. She and I have a website to share and exchange academic information about historical and scientific discoveries. A Pakistani educator contacted us about some parallel research she'd been doing and wanted us to see her findings. That's all we're here for."

"The Doctors Ramin have permits for archaeological research at Harappa and Mohenjo-Daro. But when your team arrived, they disappeared from Faisalabad, and we have no record that they ever officially checked in at the Harappa site. Can you explain that?"

"Yeah, I can *explain* that. We tried to check in at the hotel we booked and somebody started shooting up the place. We had to get out of there fast, and make sure those gunmen didn't follow us. Our friends took us home with them."

Several people at the table exchanged uncomfortable glances. The man squared his shoulders.

"We do our best to protect visitors to our country. We regret it when incidents occur that might cause them anxiety. But we cannot prevent further mishaps if we are not informed of changes of itinerary or if visitors do not at least make some effort to communicate with us. It is most unfortunate when visitors become ill or suffer injury, but travel companions must understand that we are here to help. Sometimes unfortunate incidents can be avoided with proper assistance. All we ask is to be kept apprised when travel plans change."

Keith stared at him, and at the other people. The mood of the room had changed from hostile to something suspiciously like *we're just trying to cover our tails*. Could they just be trying to figure out how to avoid blame for all these injured people? Keith gave Sophie's hand another squeeze.

"We're just waiting for our care coordinator for Dr. Ramin, my wife, and our associate to arrive, then, right?" he asked. "Now that this meeting is *over*?"

Sophie dug her nails into his palm. Keith didn't change his expression. They waited. Finally, the man at the head of the table jerked upright.

"Yes. The meeting is concluded. We do ask, since this hospital is a part of our national reputation, to be kept advised of any care-related issues while the patients remain here, before there is any further action taken. Let me repeat my assurances that we are only here to help."

Chapter Sixty-four – Holding Hands

Keith kept Sophie's hand in his and led her away from the room as quickly as possible. They stopped by Naddy's room. Keith could see from the doorway that he was awake but very groggy. The staff, seeming nervous, asked with great deference that only one visitor go in at a time.

"Let's just pray real quick, before you go in," Keith said. He did so. Sophie sniffled and didn't add anything. "You gonna be okay?" he asked her.

She patted his hand. "I will be now. Thank you. Thank you."

"God gave me the right words at the right time, I guess. That's all that happened. But anybody else tries to take you away from him, you call me. Don't budge. Just call me."

"I will." Sophie patted his face this time. "God bless you."

Keith returned to the waiting room outside the surgical unit working on Talia. David and Cindee sat stiffly, holding hands, but they jumped up when they saw him.

"What happened? Where's Sophie? Are they going to arrest us?" Cindee asked.

"Nobody's getting arrested," Keith replied. He described the meeting.

"I don't understand," David said. "It almost sounds as if they are reacting to someone asserting control over these cases from outside the hospital. Worry about their national reputation? What brought that on?"

"You think that's what it is?" Keith asked. "Who could it be? We haven't contacted the US consulate – *is* there one in Pakistan? – We didn't complain about the care, or anything. I was telling my dad how great this hospital is, and what a blessing it is to have it right here."

"Yes, but this is still so strange," David muttered. "Well, God gave you a wise response, to be sure. I still want to know if we can get any news about Jiggly."

"Do you mind if we go check, Keith? We'll just do that, and wave at Sophie, and come back as soon as we can."

"Go right ahead. I'm going to lean my head back against that wall and shut my eyes for a minute." They prayed together and Cindee and David departed.

Keith dozed in the chair but started awake to find himself alone except for a tall, forbidding-looking woman. He rubbed his eyes.

"Doctor Ewing?" Keith rubbed his eyes again, and struggled to his feet. His neck seized up but he managed to maintain eye contact while trying to rub life back into it. "What are you doing in Pakistan?"

"As long as you are surrounded by invalids, the work for the Testaments cannot continue," Dr. Ewing replied, crossing her arms. "So, this being my area of expertise, I have tasked myself with making sure they spend as little time as invalids as possible."

She held up a long, bony finger, ticking off a list. “One. Dr. Ramin is being moved out of intensive care as we speak. Two. That Italian fellow whose name I shall not attempt to pronounce is in stable condition. His arm could not be saved, and his sepsis was quite severe. It will take some time for him to heal and for the infection to clear up. He will most likely recover, though. I will see to the needed rehabilitation as soon as he is physically able to begin.

“Three. Mrs. Bradley is out of surgery, needing only some minor repair to her spleen along with treatment of a concussion and quite a number of hairline fractures. She is stable and expected to make a full recovery. You’ll be able to see her as soon as we finish here, though it may be some time before she awakens.”

“Thank you ...” Keith said uncertainly. Dr. Ewing hardly paused.

“I am arranging a medical transport to fly all of you back to Precious Treasure Campground as soon as there is no danger of setbacks for the patients. I will, as I said, personally oversee the recovery of the convalescents so that you will not be hindered when it is time to set off on the next leg of your journey.

“The new tablets have all been accounted for and are already on their way to experts for study, along with the artifacts. Initial feeling is that you and that young woman with the disturbingly green hair were correct – the Pipali artifacts are very likely to contain the keys being sought to unlock the coded messages. Your theory was applied to the work on the Ugarit tablets before the latest batch had even been received, and there are already promising breakthroughs.

“I know you have not had time to keep abreast of the latest news back home, so, with apologies for keeping you from your wife’s side, I will give you a briefing, with the emphasis on brevity. Sam has completed his inspection of the school and Brad Shannon is assisting with filing the paperwork to reopen for classes after repairs. There may be a slight delay, though, because, while the damage was not that extensive, the explosive device contained radioactive materials."

"Radioactive? A dirty bomb?"

"Yes, but the amount of radioactivity was small. Not dangerous to anyone's health. Still, as a precaution, Sam thought it best to get rid of anything likely to absorb radiation. Since the bomb was placed close to the Bible as Literature classroom, that included the students' study materials from your class."

"Of course. So now we know why they did that. Did my dad tell you about my grandfather's Bible?"

"I haven't heard anything about it."

"Grandma woke up and found a pile of dust on her bedside table. My dad has it in a freezer bag. I want to get it analyzed as soon as I can."

"I'd heard that there were traces of radiation after they scanned the Bibles," Dr. Ewing said. "Not dangerous, everyone said. You think this effect will be cumulative, though? More Bibles will disintegrate?"

"I know that if it's not already cumulative, they're going to keep sneaking in small doses of radiation until they can make that happen, if it's possible," Keith replied. "Or at least they're going to make us afraid of our own Bibles and study materials because they've been irradiated. They already succeeded at the school.

"They would've been happy if I'd been arrested over accusations that I was the bomber, or if the school got plowed under and the kids were scattered away from our influence. If more people got sicker, or even died, from radiation exposure when they worked with a ton of scanned manuscripts, that would have furthered their agenda, too, I guess."

"Who is *they,* and what is this agenda? Is it this reporter you called me about? Is she really that serious a threat? There's disagreement among the Guardians about that. Who can do what you said she claimed was her goal – to remove all access to the Scriptures and send us into spiritual withdrawal?"

Keith gave her his own tick-off list of events since they had landed in Faisalabad. Her eyes grew wider with each event. He finished off with the interrogation-style interview he had gone through with Sophie.

"They pulled Dr. Ramin away from her husband because of that? They withheld care information? Then I'm to blame for that. I may be retired, but I do still have power in the medical community, so I moved to protect you. I intended to prevent mismanagement. I had no idea that would be the reaction."

"Maybe somebody stirred the pot, by making them paranoid about your motives. It sounded like they were more scared than angry."

"I am going to urge the Guardians to take these incidents more seriously," Dr. Ewing said. "Someone certainly seems to be trying to stop this work you and your wife are doing. We are going to have to consider somehow making a wall of protection around you."

Dr. Ewing took a step toward Keith. He started to back up, but he was already supporting himself against a wall. She leaned in and kissed Keith's cheek.

"What you are doing is extraordinary," she said. "Keep doing it."

With that, she turned and left the waiting room, but called out from the doorway. "But for now, go and see your wife."

Keith slipped into the recovery room and sat beside Talia's bed. She looked even more fragile than before.

"Where's my Warrior Angel?" he whispered. "Should I get Dan in here so you can kick his butt again? I didn't even believe him when he first told that story. But I'd love to see you go warrior again. I need to see a little of that fire, Talia. Just so I know you're going to be okay."

She didn't stir, even when he held her hand and rubbed it, trailing up her bruised arm very gently. Her left arm was in a cast. They had told him it was mostly precautionary, like the boot she was going to have to wear on her right foot for a couple of weeks. He could read the report Dr. Ewing had written on Talia's case ... or at least the parts that weren't illegible because of her handwriting or the medical jargon. Talia'd had something like a concussion all over her body, was what it amounted to, partly from the explosion and partly from the knocking around trying to get to the surface. Lots of hurts in lots of places, but all of them expected to heal quickly.

Jiggly. Keith wanted to go see about him, but he didn't want to leave. Dr. Ewing had said they couldn't save his arm. How would he deal with that? Talia had said something about him saving her life. How could he have done that when he was more dead than alive? But her saying that was good enough for Keith.

"Whatever it takes, we'll take care of Jiggly."

Talia's eyes fluttered open. "How is Jiggly?" she asked.

Keith got up and kissed her forehead. "Dr. Ewing came all the way here to make sure I'm not held up by a bunch of invalids," he began, forcing a smile.

"Dr. Ewing! I had a dream that she was standing over my bed, saying, 'We'll have you up and around in no time.' I wanted to salute."

"I bet it wasn't a dream." Keith chuckled. "She really is here, and she scared the whole hospital into submission."

"I believe it," Talia said. "Ow. It hurts to laugh. Don't make me laugh."

"Okay." Keith took a deep breath. "You asked about Jiggly. So I'll tell you. They had to take his arm, and his infection is really bad, but Dr. Ewing thinks he's going to make it."

"They took his arm?" Tears ran down Talia's cheeks. "When I was fighting underwater, a whirlpool started to drag me down, but I found something to grab onto. It was Jiggly's arm. That's how he saved me, Keith."

"Don't cry, please," Keith soothed, wiping away her tears and caressing her hair. "Like I said, God does everything for His glory. Everything. Because of Jiggly's arm, you lived. And because of you, he lived."

Talia nodded slowly. Her eyes drifted shut. Keith tiptoed out into the hall and found David and Cindee waiting there.

"She was awake for a minute or so," he said. "She thought she dreamed about Dr. Ewing. Oh, maybe you guys didn't hear about her."

"We heard," Cindee said. "We met her. She even apologized for the interrogation stuff. But she still scared me."

"I will have nightmares about her. She is a woman of great power," David said. "I am glad she uses it for good."

"I told Talia about Jiggly. Have you two seen him? Any more news?"

"He's next door, there." Cindee pointed. "David went in for a second."

"He's awake, but he didn't want to talk," David said. "I can't imagine what he's going through. The first thing that went through my mind when I was shot was, *Am I going to lose my arm?* And now it's happened to him. I didn't know what to say. I tried to pray but it sounded so hollow."

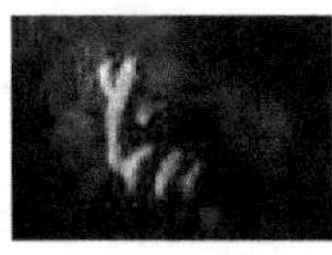

Keith went into Jiggly's room and found him staring at the ceiling. He looked so sick, and so beaten.

"If you came to read the Bible to me, or say more lame prayers like Sharon, forget it," Jiggly said in a hoarse, weak voice.

"I didn't," Keith said. "I came to thank you for saving Talia's life."

"What? I didn't save her life." Jiggly clearly tried to snarl, but it came out more of a wheeze.

"When she was drowning, she got hold of your arm and pulled herself out."

"Oh." Jiggly seemed to consider that. Talking clearly cost him a lot of effort, but between wheezing breaths and long pauses he managed to make a speech. "Well, I wasn't using it, so I guess it was okay for her to. Huh. Life's funny, isn't it? Now how can I be all bitter, when I hear something like that? How many times do we use that expression – 'I'd give my right arm for ...' whatever? Well, truth is, I would have said that about Talia. I would have done that for her, to save the Warrior Angel. So I guess that makes it okay?"

"Not really okay," Keith said. "But I hope you know I'm grateful."

"Yeah, you have cause to be," Jiggly said with a crooked grin. "You owe me bigtime, and I'll make sure and collect."

"Start collecting anytime."

"How about some of those ice chips? They tell you to sip, and go slow, and I'm – like – I can't even reach up and get the cup, and then there's a spoon, which would mean two hands , and –"

Keith grabbed the cup and the spoon off the table set over the bed. He fed Jiggly ice chips in silence for several minutes.

"I can't believe how much better that feels. I know I'm drugged up, but I'm still so dry and hot and ..."

"I can stand here all day and do this."

"Naw, you can't. How's Warrior Angel? Up kicking some butts?"

"I told her I wanted her to. Maybe tomorrow."

"So where's the next adventure? I'm ready."

"No you're not. Neither is Talia, and for sure Naddy isn't. We're taking a breather. You have a private doctor planning our trip to the States in style."

"The States? I thought they didn't let illegal aliens in?"

"What are you? Italian?"

"Well, yeah, hence the name Guglielmo."

"Dr. Ewing will figure that out."

"You mean that Iron Maiden who's taller than you are? I remember seeing her. She is mean and rough. I had to hit the morphine pump hard after she was done looking me over."

"She's not taller than me. Well ... maybe she is. But she isn't known for her bedside manner. She did promise to take good care of all my sick people. So that includes you."

"I'd rather make you my personal slave. You owe me, after all."

"I'm here as long as you need me."

"Get out of here. Your wife is gonna need you. Send Sharon back in. I owe him an apology. And Cindee. Tell her not to cry, but she and the hulking brute can wait on me, too, if they want to."

"Okay, I'll tell them."

"Naddy is gonna be okay, right?" Jiggly asked as Keith turned to go.

"Yeah, Dr. Ewing says everybody's gonna be okay. If anybody can make that happen, she can."

Chapter Sixty-five – Summer Camp

All of the rest of the hospital time and preparations for the trip were kind of a blur to Keith. David flew the plane, and he enjoyed the phony captain's monologue over the PA about mythical sights to see out the windows. Plenty of other craziness went on during the flight as he sat beside Talia in the roomy medical plane and mostly just enjoyed looking at her.

Cindee spent most of the flight in the jump seat or the co-pilot chair, at least when David was on duty. They had two co-pilots, also Drew Summers's employees, but David took the lion's share of flight time, using the excuse that he was diversifying Cindee's training.

Sophie spent the trip at Naddy's bedside. He kept protesting that he could sit up in a regular seat but Dr. Ewing shut him down. She also cast a disapproving eye backward every time Talia got up to stretch and walk around. Jiggly never stirred out of his bed, so everyone made sure to "visit" him. He complained loudly about Dr. Ewing's "mistreatment." She responded by threatening to take away his morphine button to show him real pain. It took Keith a few days to realize that those two were becoming friends of a sort.

When they arrived at Precious Treasure Campground, Keith discovered that a wing of the main "cabin" had been converted to medical and rehabilitation suites. He couldn't believe how much had happened since his and Talia's wedding. They had a couple of hundred emails from students, and had to reassure them about the rumors of death and dismemberment in Pakistan. Something seemed to have trickled out in the international news about their mishaps and a lot of reassurances were necessary. When the pleas to sign Talia's cast started coming in, they decided drastic action was in order.

"I think a summer camp is a wonderful idea," Dr. Ewing said, much to Keith's surprise. She had become unofficial Activity Director, as Jiggly expressed it, because she was so good at telling everyone what to do.

"Yeah, she's going to put black hoods on all the campers so they can't disclose the location," Jiggly snorted.

All Keith knew was that one day in August Sam Ewing arrived at the campground in an extra-long van with extra-tinted windows full of kids from Bradley Central. What followed was the most wonderful and exhausting two weeks of his life.

They had no rigid camp schedule except for Sam blowing Reveille every morning at six am, followed by prayer and flag-raising at seven. David led exercise times, including an impossible obstacle course that kept growing every day. He had a whistle he blew at random intervals, day or night, the signal for a run, a workout, some mild mixed martial arts instruction, or a "mystery activity." All of the kids tried to keep up with him. Emphasis on *tried.*

"That guy has gotta use steroids, right, Mr. Bradley?" Tom asked.

"I don't think so." Keith grinned.

Sometime between breakfast and lunch they had Bible study. It was led by a different "campground elder" each day. Afternoons they swam, canoed, hiked, mostly under Keith's supervision, or answered David's whistle. Dr. Ewing taught a pretty intensive First Aid course and she and Talia took the girls through a self-defense course. In the evenings they had more Bible study. David and Cindee also took some kids through flight simulations and gave helicopter rides.

Bart Matthews had crews to start making repairs to his abused dinosaurs, something the kids regarded as a job from heaven. They learned to work with animatronics, molded foam, and spray paint, and refused lunch and dinner one day because the T-rex would go through a thousand motions but would not lie down on its rolling framework to be loaded into a trailer after it was fully repaired and wrapped to go with a traveling exhibit.

A pizza delivery saved the day and the life-size dinosaur finally submitted. Mike and Mary, the husband and wife truckers who had helped get the Tesla and Keith and Talia to the campground, were glad to share the pizza and extremely grateful to finally get on their way to deliver the dinosaurs.

Jiggly stayed in the medical wing out of sight. Keith didn't really have time to worry about him. Besides the physical activities, he got a dozen lab partners together and set up to analyze the Bible turned to dust as well as samples of the different forms of amphibian skin and other materials they had encountered. Dr. Ewing had more access to equipment and expertise than any lab he had ever dealt with. He was able to teach the kids a ton of Science and investigative techniques while learning at least some of what he wanted to know.

Just as he and Talia were ready to collapse into bed one night, a week and a half into camp, Keith got a text message that Jiggly wanted to see him. He dragged himself away from Talia and over to the medical wing.

"What's up, Jiggly?" he asked.

"You promised to be my slave for life," Jiggly said, bundled up in blankets but sitting up on his bed. "I've hardly seen you since we got here."

"I'm sorry," Keith said. He knew this had to be some sort of con, because Jiggly had constant care, plus he was getting around pretty well and gaining strength every day. "We've been busy with the kids. You need some more ice chips, or what?"

"Well, I just thought you would like to know that soon I won't need you anymore." The blanket slipped away and Keith staggered back, seeing an elaborate metal arm mounted to Jiggly's thin torso. It reached out, extending a hand. "Let's shake on it so you know there's no hard feelings."

"What is that?" Keith gasped. He reached out to touch the flexing fingers.

"Dr. Ewing's been working on the specs since the day they took my arm off," Jiggly said, a huge grin decorating his homely face. "This isn't really attached yet. I was just messing with you."

He revealed his other hand, manipulating joystick controls under the covers. "But she's got people coming in to do the surgery first thing in the morning, so I'll be back to needing more of your fealty temporarily, I guess, and then I'll ascend to cyborg status and will need no mere mortal assistance."

"Hang on. I'm gonna go get Talia."

"Nah, it's okay. Warrior Angel needs her sleep."

"Not that bad. She needs to see this."

Talia was, in fact, already asleep, but when Keith picked her up out of the bed, blankets and all, she almost went into warrior mode on him.

"What are you doing?" she cried, pulling her fists in just in time. "Put me down!"

"C'mon. You gotta see what Jiggly's been up to."

Talia stood there, wrapped in blankets, barefooted, putting Jiggly through the paces with his arm and hand movements.

"Will it really work this well when it's part of you?" she breathed.

"If I'm a good boy, and make the therapy work, Dr. Ewing thinks so," Jiggly replied. He was squirming with excitement.

"Is she sure – really sure ... ?" Talia chewed her lip. "I mean, that it won't fail, or hurt you, or become this ... thing for you to drag around?"

"Hey, don't be such a downer," Jiggly grumbled. "Think positive."

"I'll pray hard for you," Talia said. "I wish you'd told us sooner."

"It didn't come 'til about an hour ago. I wasn't sure it was going to happen. Anyway, yeah, praying is good. But that was Dr. Ewing's 'unspoken' she said she's been making at the prayer meetings every day. She says all her prayers have been answered – how fast my infections cleared up, how good I've been healing, how I've been getting on in my therapy. She says miracles come in all shapes."

"I guess they do." Talia advanced and kissed Jiggly on the cheek. "I kept thinking – Did you lose your arm because of my grabbing onto it, making the injury worse? I'm so glad God is giving you a new one. So glad."

Jiggly went red and made the mechanical arm pat her on the back. "Didn't Keith tell you? I'd give my right arm to save you, Warrior Angel. Even this one. Go back to bed, you two."

After they had prayed with Jiggly and returned to bed, Keith and Talia lay awake a long time. "I don't know whether I'm more glad for Jiggly, or scared," Talia whispered.

"Let's just be glad. And pray. And, since we're suddenly insomniacs, I want to bounce an idea off of you. Not about Jiggly. We'll pray for him again afterwards. This is about our next adventure."

"Okay. Bounce away."

"So, we found Britomartis and her ax," Keith said, sitting up. "That was near Crete, and the Guardians have been messaging me and telling me that the city within the city in Olous really was made of artificially-grown corundum crystal. They have a theory that the corundum should have made the city pretty much indestructible. I tended to agree, and we were all still wondering why, number one, they would have built it where it would sink the way it did, and, two, how it was reduced to ruins. We wondered if the enemies had a super weapon that could penetrate the kind of force field the corundum makes.

"But, after learning about the Harappan nuclear power, and that maybe it was Pipali's people who unleashed it, I changed my idea. What if Britomartis's people had the same problem? They had to stop the enemy, whatever the cost, and their disaster plan was to destroy the city when the bad guys took it over. We came up with some kind of sound wave weapon that caused the devastation to Olous."

"Yes, that would be the way to shatter the crystalline structures," Talia agreed. "Like a high soprano can shatter a glass?"

"That's the general idea. They are experimenting with the ax, and found that swinging it hard and fast produces a tone above human hearing range. At first they had all the dogs howling within a couple miles' radius. But when they rigged up a machine that could spin it really fast, stuff started shattering. Big stuff. They had to stop testing before they ran out of high-resistance glass."

Talia giggled, then sobered. "So the ancient faithful quit running, and started fighting, but destroyed their civilizations in the process?"

"Yeah, that's the conclusion we're coming to. The Guardians are theorizing that the tone, at the right intensity, causes damage to all kinds of things, including human cells. They intend to start combing through the Gondrani and Harappan artifacts, looking to see if there's any remnant of the nuclear device they might have used to cast out the demons of Mai."

"How does this tell you where to go on our next adventure?" Talia asked.

"It doesn't," Keith replied. "Since you have more field archaeology experience than I do, I was hoping you would come up with something."

"We need to brainstorm with *Amu* and *Zanamu*," Talia replied. "Tomorrow."

Chapter Sixty-six – Where To Next?

The next morning the "camp staff" and other adults at Precious Treasure got together before Reveille and prayed for Jiggly and the campers. David, Sam, and Dr. Ewing took off and Keith and Talia opened up their brainstorming session to everyone who remained over coffee.

Everyone listened to Keith repeat what he and Talia had discussed the night before.

"We know the first Guardians of the Testaments moved into places where ancient faithful had formerly settled," Sophie replied, "but also suddenly disappeared. Guardian record-keeping was not the best; understandably, since they were fleeing to protect the tablets, just as their predecessors fled for freedom to worship the true God."

"This daughters-in-law of Noah theory you mentioned makes sense," Larry Stokes said, "given it would explain somebody thought of as a goddess, but really just a woman with a long life span and maybe other unusual genetic features. It seems like you have to find that third daughter-in-law, figure out where she settled, and you'll have the third site to search for tablets."

"The holographic map you mentioned doesn't tell you that?" Fran Taylor asked.

"The map only pointed us to Ugarit," Naddy explained. "We would not have even gotten on to the additional tablets, at Harappa and the Caves at Gondrani, if our friends with the taxi hadn't heard about Britomartis and made the connection."

Shouldn't they have enough tablets to get started, anyway, with translation or decoding or whatever it is?" Bart Matthews asked.

"Here's the problem," Keith said. "You know what it means to triangulate a position, right?"

"Yes ... I think so," Eva Sanchez said. "If you know the location of three points, you can calculate a fourth location?"

"Right," Keith said. "What we're still lacking, even if we find and decode all the tablets, is a dissemination system, for getting the message out, fast, and all around the world. We've got antennas, but we've got no transmitter."

Joshua Bradley chimed in. "I think I know where you're going with this. Once you have the three locations of the ancient faithful settlements, you'll be able to triangulate a fourth. And that's where you hope you'll find the transmitting equipment."

Talia nodded. "Even if the transmission equipment is at that third location, the home of that third daughter-in-law of Noah, we still have to find it."

"What do we do, then?" Sophie asked. "There are so many vanished civilizations, all over the world."

We must start going to each of them, looking for evidence of the third daughter-in-law of Noah," Naddy proclaimed, getting up as if he was ready to start.

Saul Taylor, who served as groundskeeper now that his cancer was in remission, said, "Can't you narrow it down, based on what you already know about the other two daughters-in-law of Noah?"

Naddy considered. "Britomartis was Minoan, one of the earliest civilizations outside of the Fertile

Crescent. Harappa is considered one of the earliest of the Indus Valley Civilizations. That is even farther outside the original area where people would have started fleeing Nimrod and other persecutors."

"We can assume they'd have to move farther and farther away to try escape the tyrants," Sophie said. "Legends talk about strangers arriving from faraway places claiming to be gods and having the power to fly, to come up out of water, and to kill massive numbers of people."

Keith nodded. "We can assume, whatever the truth in among the lies, the bad guys may have had some advanced ancient technology. Could be they stole it when they overran Noah's other faithful descendants. They ran out of people to steal from or subjugate close to home, so they spread out, searching for more slaves. They also wanted to destroy people who taught about the true God and denied the false gods."

"Maybe the third settlement would be as far away as people thought they could get," Cindee mused. "Where can we find the earliest evidence that matches elements we saw with Britomartis and Pipali – A woman as a protector, teacher, provider? Where would this third woman have to go, to keep the work of protecting and sharing the Word going?"

"A provider is a good idea," Sheila Matthews said. Maybe she was a Proverbs 31 woman – some kind of merchant."

Sophie nodded. "Her culture would have valuable trade products and evidence of interaction with others. We saw the evidences in the artifacts that seem to have messages as part of their design. They would have opportunities to share and spread the Word while hiding it in plain sight."

Talia was silent, considering. "The one thing a woman can't live without – Chocolate," she finally said, smiling at Keith.

"Chocolate?" Keith said with a grin. "Isn't that from South America?"

"Ancient Mexico," Eva corrected.

"And rubber," Naddy added. "Unique and valuable cultural contributions of the New World to ancient civilization. I think we should look into the Olmecs."

"Okay," Keith said. "Who are the Olmecs? And what kind of Mother Goddess did they have?"

"There is not much mention of women at all," Sophie admitted. "Later cultures – Aztec and Mayan – have many goddesses, but there isn't one we can certainly say was Olmec. There's so little to go on. Pottery, evidence that they used cocoa, rubber balls, and various kinds of stone and wood sculptures. Archaeologists speculate all kinds of religious practices – there are strange statues with figures that seem to be part human and part jaguar. There are also huge stone heads. Secularists are so busy attributing everything to religious practice we cannot get any objective information. Even the written language, since it is pictographic, is almost untranslated."

"There is the association with mirrors and spiders," Naddy said. "Those seem to indicate a female influence." Sophie glared at him. "What?" he asked. "What about the Spider Woman?"

"That is Aztec. Much later," Sophie said. "Don't talk foolishness."

"Perhaps the Spider Woman is an echo of an earlier leader," Naddy said. "Consider the Scripture that says, *The spider takes hold with her hands, and is in kings' palaces*. A spider's web extends her influence. She knows every movement within its sphere.

"A merchant woman could have an extensive network of contacts. She could both be warned of approaching danger, and have the means to share the message of truth. Olmec pottery has been found in many places. So have the rubber balls. They had some way of vulcanizing, all those centuries ago."

"So how would the mirrors fit into your theory?" Fran asked. "Just because women are the ones who mostly use them? A mirror is a pretty prized trade item, too, isn't it? People use them for signaling, and for other things."

"Indeed," Naddy agreed. "Again, the religious theories overwhelm any chance of learning fact. Obsidian and hematite mirrors are spoken of as being portals into the spirit world. They are often set into the eyes of the gods in later statuary."

"A mirror gives you a look at yourself," Bart said. "Like when the Scriptures say a person sees himself in a mirror, but goes his way, forgetting what he's supposed to be. Maybe that's what the mirrors were really for. To remind people to clean up their act. It's a physical picture of our spiritual need to remember God's constant presence and our responsibility to be right before Him. He can always see us. That's the true portal to another world – the connection God has chosen to make with human beings. Those people corrupted that into their false gods being able to see them, or the ability to become like them by crossing over into their world."

"That makes sense," Keith said. "Still, I'm not a big fan of calling our third daughter-in-law of Noah the Spider Woman. That sounds creepy."

"We can hold off on naming her until we're a little more certain we've found her." Talia laughed. "After all, we've already established that the Spider Woman came later. We still don't have a real Olmec woman in leadership or any other capacity."

"Not so sure Britomartis and Pipali qualify as real women, either." Keith shrugged. "We've inferred a lot about them from some images. All of this is just theory. It's the danger of persecution, and the need to prevent the Great Thirst, that we're focusing on. We need to be reasonably sure we'll find tablets where the Olmecs live before we take off."

"I may be able to help you with that," Eva said. "I'm from Mexico, remember? I got interested in the Olmec culture after the folks who were working down there rescued me. I started tracing my ancestry back, and my people lived in Veracruz, the area where the Olmecs were. There are descendants of the Olmecs who still live there, and I have contact information for them."

David popped his head in the side door, drenched in sweat and breathing hard. "The kids are ready to give up trying to catch me," he said. "Who's teaching today?"

"I am!" Joshua Bradley exclaimed, jumping up. "Thank you, David. Well, keep us posted, Mr. and Mrs. Bradley. Don't go running off too quickly. You may have forgotten, but school is starting up in about three weeks."

Keith and Talia stared at each other as the meeting broke up and the others drifted away. "School!" Keith exclaimed.

"I never even thought about starting school again," Talia said. "We need lesson plans ... ohhh!"

"We need to find out if Jiggly made it out of surgery okay first," Keith said.

"Yes. But what if we plan another trip, as soon as we're sure of where we should go, for the Bible as Literature class at Spring Break?"

"That sounds perfect." Keith kissed her, grabbed her hand, and they ran off to the hospital wing to find out about Jiggly.

Keep following the adventure in *The Great Thirst Five: Prevailing*

A Serial Archaeological Mystery

The Great Thirst

Part Five: Persevering

Mary C. Findley

Chapter Sixty-seven – School Days

Keith couldn't shake the surreal feeling of returning to Bradley Central for another school year. The place had been a second home to him all his life, but everything that had once been familiar to him had changed in the last year. Most of it seemed to be in a good way, thankfully.

The school board had been more than a little shaken by the events of last year, but an unexpected personal conference call scheduled by Dr. Williams had done much to reassure them. Keith had thought it strange that the state had switched gears from plowing Bradley Central under to reinstating everything back to the way it had been. Dr. Williams had dismissed their uncertainties with an off-handed reference to mistakes and misunderstandings. She insisted that the Bible as Literature program was alive and well, grants included.

Brad Shannon had helped the Bradleys get some compensation for the invasive and destructive search of their home. No charges had ever been filed and the search was ruled unjustified. The remodeling had included turning Joana and Keith's rooms into guest rooms where Dan, Naddy and Sophia, or any of the rest of their friends, could stay. Grandma Bradley was able to return to her senior apartments after being on the waiting list only a few weeks.

Naddy and Sophie insisted on going down to their colleagues working at an Olmec site to try to pin down whether the third daughter-in-law of Noah might really be found there. David and Cindee had announced their engagement on the last day of camp, much to the delight of the campers. They accompanied Naddy and Sophie on the trip to Veracruz about a month after school started.

Their initial findings were promising. Interviews with the local contacts Eva had suggested opened their eyes to things they had not considered before. Keith and Talia felt a little out of the loop when Sophie and Naddy remained vague about their findings, but it seemed more and more likely that they would be headed for Veracruz during Christmas vacation.

Jiggly the Cyborg, as he now preferred to be called, moved to a rehabilitation center in the "big city" where Keith had attended college. Dr. Ewing kept a watchful eye on his progress and Keith and Talia kept in touch with him too. Naddy and Sophie kept him on the payroll and promised he would be included in the search for the third daughter-in-law of Noah whenever he was ready to re-join the team.

Things began to seem almost normal to Keith as he settled into the routine of Science classes, occasional PE subbing, and Bible as Literature responsibilities. Even more kids signed up this year. They ended up starting in the auditorium when the class outgrew the largest classroom, while grant and insurance money allowed for a wall to be knocked out and a larger classroom to be built. Sam Ewing was happy to take on the task.

Keith was dimly aware that all three parents who had caused trouble last year, the Sheldons, the Holdens, and the Gregorys, were back this year, but after a month he still hadn't heard any complaining. He had to chuckle over their fears that those families were part of the conspiracy among Dr. Williams, Jenny Kaine, and the three families, to get Bradley Central shut down, or at least to stop the work of preparing for the Great Thirst.

One day as he prepared to leave school Keith got a message that Mr. Holden wanted to meet with him. "Are you sure he meant me and not my dad?" he asked the school secretary.

"I'm sure he said Mr. Keith Bradley, not Mr. Joshua Bradley," the secretary said with a smile. "They've been quiet a long time, haven't they? I guess it's time to start making a fuss again."

"Well, I do have Ruan in Earth Science this year." Keith rubbed the back of his neck. "Maybe it's about that."

"He said it was about the air filtration system," the secretary said. "And he said it was urgent. He said he'd wait in the teachers' lunch area next to the cafeteria, in case you had time to see him now. Might be best to get it over with."

"Fine," Keith sighed. "Please tell my wife where I am, and that I'll just catch a ride home with my dad."

"Hey, Mr. Holden," Keith said, shaking hands with the man as he rose from a seat in the small room off the main cafeteria. "What can I do for you?"

"I wanted to show you something," he said, producing a black plastic bag. "I'm kind of hesitant to open it, but I don't think it's really dangerous. Just ... troubling."

He undid the tie at the top of the bag and showed Keith a collection of crumbling notebooks, vinyl covers, empty spiral bindings, and parts of cards and loose papers. Most of the contents of the bag was a pile of grayish-white dust at the bottom.

"Where did you get these?" Keith asked. "Are those Bibles in there?"

"Yes, among other things," Mr. Holden replied. "My wife and I – we quit going to church years ago, before Ruan was born. But my brother is quite religious, and he leads a Bible study for some disadvantaged kids in the city. They were contacted about that Bible archiving project, or whatever it's called, that the government said it was doing, and he collected all the kids' study materials for them to scan.

"They gave him grant money to rent a better place to hold his meetings – he was able to get kitchen facilities and make some hot meals and so on for the children. He admits he and his wife didn't have a lot of money to start out with, to invest in buying the kids' supplies, so they just got cheap notebooks and five-dollar Bibles and even some used things. They stored everything in cupboards over the summer, and when he was opening up, getting ready to start up again this year, this is what he found."

Keith looked Mr. Holden in the eye. "My dad told you about the radiation we detected after the scanning crew was here last year, right?"

"Yes, but he said it wasn't likely to cause any harm. They gave out those filtration systems, with the radiation cleaners built in, as a precaution. Isn't that correct?"

"We haven't found that any *people* suffered harm," Keith replied. "But my grandfather's old Bible turned into a dust pile earlier this summer. I'm sure you heard about the ... explosion ... that went off here at the school this summer. Sam Ewing, the inspector, said he detected radioactivity and had to perform a cleanup. A lot of the student supplies left here over the summer had disintegrated and he ended up destroying everything that had been irradiated."

"Irradiated! Someone set off a dirty bomb at the school?" Mr. Holden turned white.

"It was a very low dose," Keith hastened to reassure him. "There's no danger now."

"We didn't hear anything about this. Why wasn't it all over the news?"

"I'm not sure," Keith said. "Maybe they were too busy trying to blame the bombing on me, or my wife, or my father."

"My wife told me about those rumors. In fact – Mrs. Sheldon and Mrs. Gregory and she were all saying –" He stopped and looked away. "Now look, Mr. Bradley. We may have had differences of opinion over facilities and a few complaints about policies, but we didn't come here to run you people out of town. At least, I didn't. Now, about these Bible study materials – you say another Bible has disintegrated, like these have?"

"Yeah. We've heard stories here and there about others, too, since that happened. Some people who work with really old copies of the Scriptures have said they are losing some of those, too. I suspect there are more we don't know about."

"Ruan was getting quite interested in that website over the summer – the one where the Bible study materials were scanned and stored for the government project. He annoyed my wife with all his questions, and his complaints that it didn't seem to work right most of the time.

"He was right, though. I tried to help him with it, just to stop hearing about it, and it hardly works at all. I'm curious about why you're continuing to participate in the program, if study materials are being damaged and the repository doesn't even work correctly. Is it just for the grant money?"

"We're still teaching the Bible as Literature class because we want the kids to learn the Bible," Keith replied. "People have made the same complaints about the tablets that were given to them for their participation last year. They hardly work to get on the repository site. They seem more likely to block any kind of Bible study searches than return results."

"Perhaps they're just trying to balance learning," Mr. Holden suggested. "After all, it was supposed to be a repository of all kinds of faiths, wasn't it? All kinds of knowledge?"

"My wife and I checked a lot of the religion sections on the site while making up lesson plans for this year's class," Keith replied. "Most of them aren't any more accessible than the ones about the Bible."

"Why would they set up this Religious Repository if they can't maintain access to the materials? Is the whole repository that bad?"

"No. If you want to look up information from the secularist parts of the site, those come right up. In fact, if you're not careful, almost any search will redirect you to those topics."

"I did notice that pattern when I spent some time on it with Ruan. Well, children might as well be guided away from mythology."

"So you'd prefer kids be told they're going to be able to enjoy the results of their study and hard work, and the contributions of their families and churches, preserved forever online, but instead get pushed off into something they didn't have a choice about?"

Mr. Holden bristled but his eyes settled on the contents of the black plastic bag. "Are they trying to take away people's choices? Restrict access to religious materials? Is that what this is all about? That doesn't seem right. And this radiation. What if we complained?"

"So far we haven't been able to prove any definite connection," Keith said. "I have a theory that the radiation destroying these materials has a specific signature. Unique, or at least highly identifiable. I think they're not only destroying materials, they're creating tracking markers on the ones that don't get destroyed. The tablets we were given emit the same signature. And if they are kept close to other things, those things begin to display that signature."

"The government is tracking people? Religious people? I think you're being paranoid."

"Mr. Holden, if you knew the kind of summer I just spent, I'm not sure you'd say that. I'm not sure it was the government, but I know the school was irradiated by that explosion. I know I can detect traces of radiation in my grandfather's Bible dust, other people's scanned materials, and, I'm betting, in that black bag you've got there. And I know the signatures are all the same. Besides that ..." Keith almost blurted out the whole story of Jenny Kaine, the black van, and everything that had happened in Pakistan.

Once his testing on his grandfather's Bible had been completed, and other scanned materials, they'd all discarded every Bible and tablet and notebook that had been scanned, and gotten the word out to others as well. Most hadn't listened. People were especially fascinated with the tablets, even if they didn't properly search the Repository site. They had some offline games and so-called educational activities that were very addictive. They connected to any wifi and almost always had something entertaining available.

During the summer camp, they'd confiscated several tablets during the Bible study times and found secularist mantras being taught via different kinds of games on the devices. Kids who had been sullen and uncooperative miraculously improved after a few hours without their tablets.

Keith wasn't sure he could share any of those things with Mr. Holden. Instead, after the few seconds it took for those events to click through his mind, he simply said, "Did you want me to test these for your brother?"

"No," Mr. Holden said. "Aside from your theory about signatures and dirty bombs, I think I can take your word about the cause of this destruction. Are those children in danger at that facility where they meet? Are my brother and his wife in danger?"

"Probably not," Keith admitted. "There hasn't been enough time to gauge long-term effects, though."

"Would you ... If my brother wishes to contact you, are you open to that?"

"Absolutely." Keith scribbled his phone number down and handed it to Mr. Holden. "Anytime."

The Edge Books

He said to her, "Woman, where are those accusers of yours? Has no one condemned you?" She said, "No one, Lord." And Jesus said to her, "Neither do I condemn you; go and sin no more." Then Jesus spoke to them again, saying, "I am the light of the world. He who follows Me shall not walk in darkness, but have the light of life." (Jn 8:10-11 NKJ)

Find Out More

On Twitter https://twitter.com/TheEdge_Books

Our Site www.TheEdgeBooks.blogspot.com

On Facebook
https://www.facebook.com/TheEdgeBooks

And Pinterest
http://www.pinterest.com/lmarshall41/the-edge/

The best gift you can give an author

is an honest, thoughtful review. Please consider leaving one online. Help us understand what you liked and didn't like about the book and why. Help authors reach more readers and spread your influence and ours. If you liked the book, please recommend it to your spouse, friends, pastors, teachers, cashiers, employers, – anybody and everybody you see each day. If you don't know what to say, remember Proverb 16:3 – Commit thy works unto the Lord and thy thoughts shall be established. Thank you!

OTHER BOOKS AND PRODUCTS FROM FINDLEY FAMILY VIDEO PUBLICATIONS

All our books (including Historical Fiction, SciFi, contemporary relationships short stories, and an Archaeological Mystery serial) are linked on our blog.

Elk Jerky for the Soul includes posts on current issues, excerpts from our fiction and nonfiction works, Bible teaching, travel and everyday observations, and more. http://findleyfamilyvideopublications.com/

Visit our YouTube Channel https://www.youtube.com/channel/UCGhwNpU115ARMwgYwTIJBrA/featured. Book trailers, video excerpts, project teasers, and more. Science, History, Literature, and biblical worldview studies are the focus of our book and video projects.

Historical Fiction

by Michael J. Findley

The Ephron the Hittite Series (Including boxed set of all titles)

Ephron Son of Zohar

Tawananna Daughter of Zohar

Heth Son of Canaan Son of Ham, Noah

Shelometh Daughter of Yovov Wife of Ephron

Zita Son of Ephron and Shelometh

Adult Romantic Suspense

by Mary C. Findley

The Men of the Realmlands series

Book One: The Baron's Ring

Book Two: The Captain's Blade

Send a White Rose

Chasing the Texas Wind

Carrie's Hired Hand (novella)

Young Adult Historical Adventure

by Mary C. Findley

Hope and the Knight of the Black Lion (plus illustrated version)

The Benny and the Bank Robber Series

Benny and the Bank Robber (Plus homeschool editions for student and teacher with review and vocabulary)

Doctor Dad

The Oregon Sentinel

Lines in Pleasant Places

Science Fiction and Fantasy

by Michael J. Findley

The Empire Saga (all six of the following books in one volume)

City on a Hill and Sojourner (Combined Novella and Short Story)

Nehemiah LLC (Full-length novel available as a standalone ebook, paperback, and hardcover versions)

Empire One: Humiliation

Empire Two: Repentance

Empire Three: Sanctification

Steampunk

by Sophronia Belle Lyon (pen name for Mary C. Findley)

The Alexander Legacy Steampunk Literary Tribute Series

Book One: A Dodge, a Twist, and a Tobacconist (including illustrated version)

Book Two: The Pinocchio Factor

Book Three: The Most Dangerous Game

Book Four: Beware the Bustle

Fantasy/Allegory

by Mary C. Findley

Allegorical clockwork novella inspired by Little Red Riding Hood

The Acolyte's Education

A Paranormal Urban Fantasy serial

His Sign: The Wait Is Over

His Sign 2: The Ezra Solution

Contemporary Fiction

by Mary C. Findley

Romantic Suspense Novella

Fall On Your Knees

Relationships Short Stories

Fifty Shades of Faithful

Fifty Shades of Faithful 2: In Living Color

The Great Thirst Serial Archaeological Mystery (including boxed set of all titles)

Part One: Prepared

Part Two: Purified

Part Three: Pursued

Part Four: Persecuted

Part Five: Persevering

Part Six: Protected

Part Seven: Prevailing

Murder Mystery

Mapped Out Murders

Nonfiction

by Mary C. Findley

Write for the King of Glory, 2nd Edition (updated, with tips on indie writing and publishing)

by Michael J. and Mary C. Findley

The Good, the Bad, and the Ugly: A Readers' and Writers' Guide for Believers

Biblical Studies (Teacher and student editions plus excerpts in OT and NT Manuscript History)

Antidisestablishmentarianism (illustrated and plain versions)

Serial versions, illustrated and plain

What Is an Establishment of Religion?

What Is Secular Humanism?

What Is Science?

What Are the Results of the Establishment of Secular Humanism?

The Conflict of the Ages series (All have teacher and student editions plus one combined teacher edition for 1-3)

I. The Scientific History of Origins

II. The Origin of Evil in the World that Was

III. They Deliberately Forgot: The Flood and the Ice Age

IV. Ice Age Civilizations

V. The Ancient World

by Michael J. Findley

Short Recaps of longer nonfiction works (Antidisestablishmentarianism and Conflict of the Ages)

Disestablish: An Overview from Creation to the Ice Age

Under the Sun: The Truth about History from the Beginning

*****

Christian Books in Multiple Genres. Join Christian Indie Author ~ Readers Group on Facebook. https://www.facebook.com/groups/291215317668431/

www.ingramcontent.com/pod-product-compliance
Lightning Source LLC
LaVergne TN
LVHW050551160826
845677LV00011B/2275

* 9 7 9 8 2 3 0 2 9 6 4 9 2 *